I0596205

WRAPPED UP WITH YOU

PACIFIC VISTA RANCH BOOK FOUR

CLAIRE MARTI

For Kim...this one is for you, my beautiful, hilarious, forever friend

CHAPTER 1

Rafael Cruz strode down the bright white hallway toward his boss's office, brainstorming about the critical evening ahead. His boss had booked an entire table at the Jingle Ball at Rancho Valencia, one of the fanciest resorts in North San Diego County. Not only was the firm's contribution helping benefit the Testicular Cancer Awareness Foundation, but tonight, Rafael had the opportunity to land not one, but two new clients for Trident Wealth Consultants.

His lips curved up--nothing like combining a good cause with his ambition. He'd played an instrumental role in convincing two of the firm's major clients, the Harmons and Blakes, to invite their ultra-wealthy friends who were considering a new wealth management team. After all, he'd been managing their fortunes for a few years now and they were thrilled with his performance. Next year when MacDonald retired, he'd be first in line to run the business.

After a triumphant night, he had an excellent weekend planned to meet a few buddies to surf Torrey Pines in the morning plus a date with the hot little brunette he'd met in line at his favorite lunch spot yesterday. Life was pretty damn perfect.

His ebullient mood burst when he saw *her* lurking in front of MacDonald's closed office door. Ever since Ms. Phoebe Hollingsworth--seriously, could she have a more British Lady of the Manor name?--had started working at his firm three months ago, she'd rubbed him the wrong way. With her conservative straight-laced dresses, severe bun, and glasses, she looked like she belonged in the stacks of an ancient university, not in a Southern California wealth management firm. Did the woman even notice the office's floor-to-ceiling windows showcasing the pristine blue sky or did she keep her nose buried in work 24/7?

Hadn't someone given her the memo that she lived in the land of sunshine, surfers, and casual wealth?

Since Ms. Ice Queen hadn't noticed him yet, he raked his gaze from the top of her burnished golden-red updo, down the severe lines of her white-collared gray sheath dress, along with--whoa. How had he never noticed her mile-long legs before? Fire-engine red pumps with pointed toes, a sexy low side cut, and skinny high heels showcased defined calves. Had she always worn killer shoes like that? Totally not the low-heeled sensible shoes he'd expected to match her prim nun's outfit.

Most of the time, he found that the second she started speaking, her cool, pompous voice grated on him, and he'd simply tune her out. He didn't have time to be spoken down to--his focus in the office was on business. But, damn, those shoes instantly created the vision of her digging them into his back as he wrapped those long legs around his waist. He sucked in a breath and the back of his neck heated.

Where the hell had that image come from? He shook his head. No way in hell was this snooty woman usurping his role at Trident. Even though she was new to the company, she'd brought in enough big clients and was showing impressive enough returns to have turned the heads of everyone, especially his boss'. It was clear she was his main competition for the promotion.

Her head lifted. "What are you doing here?" Unusual silver-gray eyes froze him from behind her dark-framed glasses.

He gritted his teeth. "If you haven't noticed, Ms. Hollingsworth, I work here." He just couldn't seem to call her by her first name, which was weird.

She rolled her eyes. "Don't worry, everybody notices you, *Mr. Cruz*. I meant what are you doing here at Mr. MacDonald's office? I've got a meeting with him in…" She flicked a glance at the sensible stainless-steel watch on her narrow wrist, "thirty seconds. So why don't you flit off and come back later?"

Rafe counted to three before responding. Oh yes, this was why he'd never noticed her legs, much less her shoes. Because she couldn't seem to speak to him without dripping condescension. Sarcasm was one of his own favorite forms of communication, but this woman elevated snark to a whole other level.

"Alright, Bitter Betty Table for One, dial it back. I'm meeting with MacDonald now. You must be confused." He congratulated himself on his even, almost charming tone.

Her lips parted and her eyes narrowed. "Confused? I––"

The enormous door whipped open and they both jolted. "I thought I heard voices. Rafe, Phoebe, excellent, you're both here. Come on in and have a seat. We don't have much time." Their boss strode back to his massive, sleek modern desk and sat.

They exchanged glances, both of their expressions now impassive as they followed him to sit in the matching charcoal gray armchairs facing the desk. Rafe refused to allow his boss to see his annoyance and, apparently, she was an expert at appearing unruffled.

"Is there an emergency? Something you need me to handle before this evening?" Rafe asked. Saving the day was one of his top talents and, again, no way was Ms. Phoebe Hollingsworth stealing the show with her measured tones and cool controlled demeanor.

Out of his peripheral vision, he caught her full, pink lips compressing into a tight line before she spoke. "What can I do to help?" He had never noticed how full her lower lip was before. Probably because she usually looked like she was sucking on a lemon.

MacDonald rested his chin on his steepled fingers, and his piercing blue eyes studied them. "I need both of you to step up tonight. I can't attend the event after all, so you two will be representing the firm and courting the potential new clients. We need to review the research we've completed on the prospects and then I need to know I can count on you to close the deal tonight."

PHOEBE'S FINGERS curled around the edges of her tablet and her pulse kicked up a notch. Her boss wanted her and *Mr. Perfect* to attend the Ball together and work as a united team? How in the world would she be able to endure hours of looking at his thick, shiny, dark hair that always fell just so across his broad forehead or his perfect square jaw with a hint of cleft in his strong chin or those damn thick, dark eyelashes framing penetrating whiskey brown eyes? And that was before he spoke in that smooth husky baritone.

Not that she'd spent time studying him or anything, but he was just so in your face with his tall, leanly muscled frame stalking all over the office like a panther. At 5'10 herself, she often was eye to eye with the mostly male members of her profession, but even in her favorite heels, he still seemed to loom over her. Not that he ever noticed her presence. His ability to ignore her, even when she was leading meetings, wasn't exactly subtle.

On her first day of work, his gaze had skimmed over her dismissively, like she was a new computer or a damn lamppost. She'd been nervous that day––not about the career opportunity, which she relished––but worried he might recognize her. Nope, it was if he had zero recollection of meeting her at Harvard and probably hadn't bothered to look at her credentials to learn they'd attended the same graduate business program. Kind of humiliating when she'd crushed on him from afar at school, observed him dating every other pretty, smart girl on campus, and even now he remained oblivious to her.

Not that she'd wanted to be noticed by the player who not only scored all the top grades and honors, but scored with every woman at whom he flashed that wicked grin. Granted, work was always her number one priority. She'd fought hard to earn the scholarships to undergrad and graduate school.

And now, of all the boutique wealth management firms in Southern California, she'd ended up in the same company. It was bad enough having to work in the same four-thousand-square-foot office and see him once a week for meetings. And Mr. Perfect seemed to always be flirting or laughing or schmoozing someone. He hadn't changed a bit over the last few years. Still strutting around like he owned the place with women falling at his feet.

She didn't have time for players or hell, even nice guys. No, until she'd achieved her goals, men could wait. Not like she didn't date here and there, but when guys realized she worked an average of seventy hours a week, they disappeared. They might claim they wanted a woman with her own life, but when confronted with her job and her weekend tennis matches, there just wasn't much time for romance.

How "Mr. 40 Under 40 Eligible Bachelor" managed to earn his reputation as one of the best wealth managers in the country and still have a different woman on his arm every week was a mystery. Jerk.

"Of course." Phoebe flipped open her tablet. "I've got their files right here. I'm confident I'll be able to connect with them, especially the Samuels, since they're both also Southerners and University of Virginia alumni."

"You're from the South?" Rafael asked, doubt in his deep baritone.

She glanced at him. "Yes." Not that anyone would ever hear the slight twang she'd ruthlessly trained out of her voice once she'd left Tennessee.

"That's excellent, Phoebe. I knew that would be a great commonality. I know how you Wahoos are about school pride. And Rafe, I'm sure you know that the Levines are avid surfers and take surf vacations around the world. Both couples have fortunes comparable to our current clients and I think they are both excellent fits for our style and strategies."

Rafe nodded and started to speak, but Cliff held up one deeply tanned hand.

Their boss stared between them again, his gray brows drawn together over a hawk-like nose. "I'm apprehensive about not joining you this evening, however, and need some reassurance from both of you."

Phoebe's brows rose and she couldn't help but notice Rafe's dark brows winged up too. What kind of concern could he possibly have? Although she thought Mr. Perfect was a pompous ass, he had an excellent track record at work. She might dislike his demeanor, but she couldn't deny his success. And his work ethic couldn't be as superficial as his personal life if he'd earned his MBA with honors. Just like she had.

"Look, I'll be frank. You two are the smartest advisors I've had the pleasure to work with in my career. That's why I hired you both. And next year, when and if I do decide to retire and play golf every day, one of you may be taking the helm of the firm. But." He shook a finger at them.

Phoebe preened under his praise, easily ignoring the part about *him*. "But?" She'd never found an objection she couldn't turn around and certainly wouldn't start doing so now. Not when the dangling carrot of managing a firm was close enough that she could take a bite of it. She'd sacrificed her personal life to establish her impeccable reputation in the male-dominated industry and relocated to California for the opportunity to run Trident one day.

"Look, you two are professionals and I have the utmost faith in your work. But it hasn't escaped my notice that you don't get along."

Crap.

Rafe chuckled. "Cliff, that's not true. I just don't see Ms.— I mean Phoebe, around very often. We're both just really busy. Right, Phoebe?" He turned to her, his eyes gleaming.

Phoebe shrugged a shoulder and forced her lips to curve upward. "Rafael's right. There's no issue." Her toes strained to cross in her pumps at the blatant lie. Sometimes honesty was not the best policy. She couldn't afford for her boss to question her professionalism.

Clifford J. MacDonald raised his eyebrows. "Look, I've noticed the tension between you and the staff mentioned some type of scuffle in the kitchen? If there is a problem, let's clear it up right now. We can't afford to have a hint of dissension in front of these clients tonight."

A pit formed in Phoebe's belly. Crap, someone had not

only heard their rude little exchange in the kitchen last month, but reported back to their boss. Over the years, she'd crafted her conservative, proficient image and nothing ruffled her. Nothing. Except for this man next to her who was now a threat to her career?

And he'd been the one who started it when he'd made a snide comment about her brewing tea. Something about teatime with the Queen or some such nonsense. Of course she'd retorted about his habit of frothing all the milk for his fancy cappuccinos. But that wasn't such a big deal, was it? With clients present she'd be able to refrain from responding to his childish comments. But how embarrassing to be called out about it. All Mr. Perfect's fault. She hadn't gotten this far in a cutthroat industry to be held back now because of him.

"Cliff, really, there is no problem and both Ms. Hol--I mean Phoebe--"

Clifford threw up his hands. "That right there is not acceptable. What is going on with you not calling her by her first name? Did you two date at Harvard or something? What's the deal?"

Rafe turned to look at her, his dark brows up to his hairline. "Harvard? You went to Harvard?"

At this rate, her tablet would disintegrate in her hands she was clutching it so tight. Too bad it wasn't his neck. "Yes, I graduated a year behind you. You must not keep up with the alumni network." *Jerk.*

Cliff shook his head. "Okay, not Harvard. Look, you two actually have a lot in common. One thing that attracted me to both of you was that you'd both gone to school on academic scholarships. Your work ethics are impeccable. I don't have a clue why you seem to dislike each other and frankly, I don't give a damn. I care about this firm and these clients. So, you will figure out this situation. You will be charming, professional, and show how Trident has advisors who work together as a team. Got it?"

Rafael had also been on scholarship? Phoebe nodded, her heart now galloping in her chest. "Of course, Cliff, we'll be a united front and I'm confident the prospects will come on board. Right, Rafael?" She shifted in her seat and smiled congenially at Mr. Perfect. Good thing their boss couldn't see her eyes boring into him. If she were Medusa, he'd be stone.

"Of course, *Phoebe*." Rafe emphasized her first name with a wicked grin. "In fact, why don't we meet a little early at The Pony Room. It's the bar at Rancho Valencia upstairs from The Terrace Ballroom where the Jingle Ball is being held. We can have a drink and get to know each other a little better. See how much we have in common."

Extra time together? Just the two of them? Heat flared in Phoebe's belly. His smooth voice evoked images of raw, passionate sex. Long-fingered hands and sensual lips capturing her own. And time to squash that little fantasy until it disappeared.

"That's a great plan, Rafael." She looked up at Mr. MacDonald. "Trust me, sir, tonight will go off without a hitch and the clients will believe we're not just colleagues but friends."

Clifford studied them and his lips twitched. "Don't let me down. And enjoy yourselves. It's my favorite charity event of the holiday season, maybe even the year."

When it was clear they were dismissed, Phoebe rose from the chair and prayed her face didn't give her away. "I'll report back tomorrow."

He shook his head. "Tomorrow is Saturday and I'm leaving town for the holiday. The office is closed until the Monday after New Years. We can discuss it then."

Rafe stood and they crossed to the door together. Her skin tingled from their proximity and his masculine scent, coffee and a hint of the ocean, teased her. *Keep walking, girl, and act like nothing is wrong.*

When Rafael closed the door behind them, both their professional masks disappeared.

"I can't believe we got reprimanded because of your childish comments about me drinking tea in the afternoon. Way to go, Cruz." Phoebe whispered.

"Oh please, *Phoebe*," he drew out the syllables into a faux British accent, "Look, I can act professional. Maybe if you weren't so damn snotty all the time, I wouldn't have made a joke."

She gasped. "Me? Are you kidding me? You with your--"

He grasped her arm and led her away from their boss's office. "Keep your voice down, for god's sake. I'm not going to let your attitude screw up my promotion next year. So, this is how it's going to be. You'll meet me at 5 p.m. sharp at The Pony Room. Take a cab. I've got the limo coming to take us home after the Ball. We will interview each other-- favorite color, school stories, family stories--we will be the best of friends for the clients tonight. Got it?" He spoke through a clenched jaw.

Phoebe shook off his grip and squared her shoulders. "Got it. Just make sure you'll be able to keep your focus on the table tonight. No hooking up with random chicks." *Ha, take that.*

A small tic appeared in his lean cheek. "Were you saving that up all day? I'll see you later. Try to look festive and not like you're headed to a convent." His gaze raked down her length and with that he turned on his heel and strode down the hall.

Phoebe's fingers curled into fists. Oh, a convent, huh? Was Mr. Perfect in for a bombshell tonight.

CHAPTER 2

Rafe checked the entrance of Rancho Valencia's famous Pony Room entrance again. No irritating Ice Queen in sight. Only the Rancho Santa Fe elite clustered around the smooth golden marble bar, clad in their holiday finery. Tasteful instrumental holiday tunes melded with lively chatter and bursts of laughter. Standing room only.

Fortunately, he was a regular, and his favorite bartender had reserved him a low, dark mahogany table in the corner near the enormous glass patio doors. He settled into the butterscotch leather chair, sampled the rich Cabernet Sauvignon, and admired the twinkling lights and potted poinsettias that adorned the packed bar.

The distinct clicking of heels on the polished hardwood floor drew his attention. Sounded similar to Ms. Hollingsworth's gazelle-like stride. Why the hell he recognized her walk wasn't something he cared to analyze. But where was she?

A flash of scarlet caught his eye and he gulped a sip of wine to quench the sudden drought in his throat. A woman in a floor-length red dress wove her way through the crowd.

Every step revealed flashes of toned ivory leg via a thigh-high slit. Who was this goddess? His gaze traveled up a shapely slender form showcased in ruby red silk and his jaw dropped. It couldn't be…

A cloud of titian curls floated around toned shoulders and delicate collarbones. When their eyes met, his entire body turned to stone in an instant. The Ice Queen was more fiery temptress tonight. Her face was a perfect oval and somehow her glasses emphasized the high slash of her cheekbones. What the hell?

This was Phoebe Hollingsworth?

She reached the table, her full scarlet lips curved into a smirk, clearly savoring his reaction. "Hello, Rafael. So kind of you to get us a table. This place is a zoo."

In a daze, he rose to his feet and reached to pull out her chair. Sparks shot up his arm when his fingers brushed her hand. She snatched her hand back, sat down, and crossed one mile-long leg over the other, exposing another tantalizing glimpse of creamy thigh.

His adjusted in his chair, his pants now uncomfortably tight. *Holy hell.* "No problem. What can I get you to drink? They have excellent cocktails or champagne or…?"

She raised one auburn brow. "If you're drinking Cab, I'll have a glass, please."

She might resemble a siren tonight, but her voice was all business. As usual.

Rafe resisted the urge to roll his eyes--he'd warm her up if it killed him. Nothing would screw up landing the new clients. "Our first thing in common. It is Cab and it's excellent." He lifted two fingers at the cocktail waitress with a quick grin.

Ms. Hollingsworth's--*damn it*--Phoebe's lips tightened, but she didn't make her usual snarky remark. A Christmas miracle. "Let's get started. In the interest of time, I prepared a list of questions." She unclasped a tiny silver purse and fished out a piece of paper.

He bit back a bark of laughter but managed to answer. "A list?" His mother had drilled manners into him and his brother Jake from the time they could talk. He'd be polite.

"Oh, do you have a better way of keeping track? A little black book, maybe?" Her brows winged up again. "Now, first we both earned our MBAs from Harvard, you a year ahead of me. And we both went on scholarship. Why don't you tell me more about your family?"

He sighed and prayed wine would relax her uptight posture. "Grew up right here in San Diego, dad is a chef, mom stayed home to raise my younger brother and me. Jake is a firefighter and recently got married to an equine vet named Amanda. They live out here in Rancho Santa Fe. I run and surf for fun."

She pushed her glasses back up on the bridge of her nose and consulted the list again. "Favorite drink? Food? Movie? Book?"

"Do you do this on first dates?" No surprise why she was single. She *was* single, right? His gaze slid to her left hand, and her third finger was bare. He kicked himself––he always learned about his co-workers because they were a team, but for some reason had avoided doing so with her.

She wrinkled her small nose. "Last I checked, tonight is a business event where we have the opportunity to land enormous clients. But I bet you don't ask any questions on dates, do you? Just talk and talk until it's time to take home the flavor of the night?" Her tone was sticky sweet.

His nostrils flared and he tamped down on the irritation flashing through him. "Actually, my *conversations* are generally two-sided. But by all means, let's continue with the interrogation. Please, tell me all about yourself."

She narrowed icy silver eyes, her fiery cloud of hair

gleaming under the overhead chandelier lights. "Fine. I love anything Italian––especially pesto pasta, margherita pizza, Barbera and Nebbiolo wines, and Nutella gelato. I play tennis every weekend and I'm fabulous. I grew up a tomboy, with three older brothers."

The waitress appeared and Phoebe paused long enough to thank the server and sample the wine. "And this wine is excellent."

He inclined his head. "You've got great taste. I love wine too, Italian included. So how did we never meet at Harvard? I would have remembered you." Three brothers could explain the sheen of toughness she exhibited. And what he'd assumed was condescension could simply be her intelligence and drive at work. Because this woman was more intriguing than icy.

That eyebrow flew up again. "We didn't have any classes together. Your, um, reputation preceded you, so I knew who you were. We crossed paths, but you never noticed. Kind of like at the firm." She shrugged one slender shoulder. "Anyway, if we both survived the Haah-vaad snob brigade as scholarship students, I think we can handle a social evening."

The back of his neck tightened. Damn, she wasn't too far off base. It was too bad she'd been subjected to the pretentious attitude of the wealthy students who peered down their aristocratic noses at the "free-riders" too.

He swallowed. "Yes, we can. But it's not like you go out of your way to attract attention. And since you went to UVa undergrad, does that mean you're from Virginia?"

Her mouth––that tempting mouth––tightened for a moment and her warm expression cooled. "No, I grew up in a tiny town in Tennessee, near the border."

The prim and proper Phoebe was from small town Tennessee? "You don't have an accent. Hell, I figured you were from the Northeast."

"I left Tennessee when I was 17, so the accent disappeared. Everyone in my family is in education. I'm the anomaly. When I knew I wanted to go into finance, I may as well have said I wanted to be an astronaut." She gazed down and adjusted her glasses.

"Yes. I hear you on the anomaly. I was the first person in my family to go to college." No need to go into family dynamics tonight. "I almost didn't recognize you tonight.

Her eyes widened. "Seriously? Because my hair is down?"

Damn it, he hadn't meant to insult her. "It's not just your hair. You look stunning." Mouthwatering even.

"At least you got to the compliment eventually. And you look very handsome." Her tongue flicked out and moistened her plump red lips before setting down her glass.

He fingers gripped his glass hard and he tamped down the arousal surging through him. She'd basically called him shallow, and he still wanted to wrap his hands in all that hair and see if she tasted as delicious as she looked. But he hadn't achieved his pinnacle of success by acting like a reactionary teenager. Tonight was business.

"Thanks. Now should we divide and conquer with the Samuels and Levines or play it by ear and let it unfold naturally?" He asked.

"Let's focus on building relationships. The Blakes invited them and I'm sure the prospects have done their due diligence on the firm. At this point, let's just make sure they have a good time tonight and if they bring up business, we go there." She inclined her head.

He flashed a grin. "Look at us, agreeing and everything. This truce isn't too tough."

Her lips curved upward in the first genuine smile she'd ever bestowed on him. "We're regular besties now. And who knows, maybe we can even extend it to work on Monday."

He held up his hands and laughed. "Don't get all wild and crazy on me now. One evening at a time."

She rolled her eyes, but grinned back. "Anyways, should we head downstairs?"

Rafe pulled out his money clip and tucked some cash underneath his wineglass. "Let's do this. This one's on me." He rose from the table.

She gracefully stood, almost eye to eye with him in her strappy stilettos.

Business, Cruz, don't forget tonight is business.

CHAPTER 3

*P*hoebe dug into her reserves of cool, calm, and collected as she and Rafe descended the stairs to the Jingle Ball. Despite wanting to take a bite out of his sinful lower lip and slide her fingers into his tousled dark chocolate colored hair, tonight she would strike the perfect balance between competent professional and friendly colleague. Somehow, one on one he wasn't such an arrogant jerk, but that made him even more dangerous. Plain and simple. She'd submit to a full leg wax before ever admitting her attraction to him.

Even though learning he'd been the first kid in his family to go to university and he'd also needed a scholarship softened her harsh view of him a teeny bit. He was famous for his charm and in just mere minutes, her own defenses had lowered and she'd almost forgotten how rude he'd been to her since she'd arrived in California. Not to mention his sheer lack of acknowledging she was alive back in Cambridge.

Her ultra-skinny heel snagged on the broad terracotta tiled stairs and she stumbled right into Rafe's lean muscular frame, one hand grasping for purchase and landing on firm, defined pectorals. The fine hairs on the back of her neck rose--every inch of her leaping to attention. A powerful arm slid around her waist and steadied her. Goosebumps leapt up on her bare shoulders and heat flared in her belly. She yanked her hand back like she'd been branded. *Holy smokes.*

Rafe's jaw clenched at her dramatic withdrawal. "Don't worry, I'm not hitting on you. And you should have brought a jacket, half this resort is outdoors."

And there he was--Mr. Dismissive. "That would have been helpful information before. And don't worry, I know your usual type." At least he thought her goosebumps came from the weather and not her reaction to his touch. She still wasn't used to the way warm California days cooled into crisp evenings.

He hissed out a breath. "Just try to stay balanced in those stilts. And I see the Harmons in the doorway, so remember. We're the dream team." He bared his teeth at her in what might pass for a smile from a distance. A ten-mile distance.

She rolled her eyes. Had she really thought they could get along? "More like nightmare. But I want these clients and so do you. Go time." She softened her jaw and allowed her lips to curve into a small smile. She would be professional if it killed her.

The Harmons—a tall, lanky, silver-haired man and his petite brunette wife standing in front of an arched doorway —caught sight of them and waved. Phoebe matched Rafael's long stride as they approached.

"Hello there, Rafe. And who's your lovely date tonight?" Mrs. Harmon beamed at them.

Phoebe's spine stiffened. Although she hadn't met these clients yet, didn't they know she worked with Rafe? Not an auspicious start to the evening.

Rafe threw back his head and laughed. "Oh, Shannon and

Steve, I didn't realize you hadn't met Trident's newest advisor. This is Phoebe Hollingsworth, we were at Harvard together."

Phoebe pinned a smile on her face. "It's nice to meet you Shannon, Steve. I'm looking forward to enjoying Jingle Ball with you." They shook hands.

"Oh, I'm sorry, my dear. Although if I were twenty years younger, I wouldn't mind being mistaken for Rafe's date." Shannon waggled her eyebrows.

It wasn't a big deal, but just because it was Mr. Perfect, she struggled to soften her stiff jaw and appear unperturbed.

"Shall we head inside? Our table is up front by the stage." Mr. Perfect was smooth and charming as he guided them through the door.

When they stepped into the ballroom, Phoebe's eyes widened. Strand upon strand of tiny lights glittered from the ceiling and chandeliers. The ballroom opened out onto a patio where an enormous Christmas tree sparkled, and more lights twinkled like stars. White-cloth covered tables with poinsettia centerpieces and sumptuous crystal and china place settings filled out the space. The expansive room was breathtaking in all its holiday splendor.

Already the ballroom was more than half-full and black and white clad servers circled about with trays of champagne and hors d'oeuvres. They crossed the noisy room to join their group already seated at the round table centrally placed next to the stage. Lively familiar holiday tunes contributed to the bustling atmosphere.

After introductions, Phoebe found herself sitting to the right of Rafael. The seating arrangements were snug, so his muscular thigh was mere inches from her bare skin. Her acting skills would need to be Oscar-worthy tonight to pretend they were work buddies. Not to mention to mask her chemical reaction to him.

Rob Samuels, one half of her "assigned" couple, shouted over the enormous flower centerpiece. "So, Phoebe, I understand you're also a Wahoo. What brought you out to California?"

Although Rafe was chatting with Ella Levine to his left, Phoebe was inches away from him and could almost see his ear perk up. Now he was curious about her?

"I was working in New York and came out here for a business trip. Let's just say I didn't want to leave. I was fortunate enough to connect with Mr. MacDonald and here I am."

Between the music and a few hundred chattering guests, Phoebe practically bellowed into the jagged crimson leaves that obscured half of Rob's face. Whoever had designed these centerpieces obviously hadn't considered group logistics.

"San Diego is hard to leave. Will you be flying back to the east coast for the holidays or is MacDonald keeping you chained in the office?" Sasha Blake yelled from her seat.

Okay, this was getting ridiculous. Before she could solve the issue, Rafe stood, plucked up the super-sized holiday bush, and carted it over to a banquet server poised near the arched doorway. The wide-eyed young blonde nodded and accepted the plant from him. He flashed his sexy grin and strolled back to the table. So, Rafael was a man of action.

Sasha lifted her champagne flute. "Cheers to Rafe for always coming up with a quick solution. We'd have been shouting at each other all night. So Phoebe?"

The group immediately felt more cohesive and Phoebe relaxed into the comfortable chair before responding. "I usually spend Christmas with my family, but this year I'm staying here." Although she'd never spent the holiday alone and hated not seeing her parents and brothers, her desire to excel at Trident Wealth took precedence.

Conversation now flowed naturally around the table and she grudgingly admitted to herself that Rafe's charm and expertise impressed her. Without their personal feelings complicating matters, they bounced around ideas about everything from holiday plans to market predictions seamlessly between the current and prospective clients.

"I can't believe you've only been with Trident a few months, Phoebe. You and Rafe are natural partners, like you've been working together for years. Were you close in business school too?" Ella Levine leaned over and asked.

Phoebe froze and Rafe stiffened next to her. She waved a hand in the air. "Rafe's easy to work with for anyone, I think. But I was a year behind him at Harvard and I'm afraid he didn't know I was alive." Her tone was light, but her shoulders tensed--why did that still bother her?

Rafe patted her arm and chuckled. "I doubt if either of us knew everyone in the program—too busy with study groups and books. But I've really enjoyed getting to know Phoebe."

Phoebe bit the inside of her lip to prevent snorting. He always had an answer for everything--"enjoyed getting to know her"--*yeah, right.* He'd never even called her by her first name until today, if he'd even known what it was. And in Cambridge he'd been too busy flirting with every woman except for her.

She smiled and sipped her wine. There were eight other people at the table to focus her attention on. Time to dig deeper with the Samuels and establish more rapport. She'd simply ignore Rafael. Because she'd been doing such a spectacular job so far.

"So Rafe, have you been able to buy that restaurant for your talented father yet? If you're looking for investors, we're definitely interested." Tim Blake said and his lovely wife Sasha nodded.

Phoebe whipped her head toward Rafael. "You're buying your dad a restaurant?"

He shrugged nonchalantly. A flush crept up the back of

his neck, but even in the muted light from the chandelier, it was visible. "Not yet, but I'll let you know."

Something melted in her chest. Okay, that was seriously sweet. To not only be the first one in his family to attend college, but to buy his chef dad a restaurant. Not exactly a token gift. Perhaps she'd been hasty judging Rafael and assuming all his relationships were as superficial as his love life.

The evening began to fly by in a blur of delicious wine pairings with each increasingly decadent course of the meal. Phoebe found herself laughing and joking with everyone, even Rafe. *Especially* Rafe. Awareness danced along her skin from their proximity.

Listening to his intelligent conversation, enjoying the smoothness of his rich voice, and trying not to jump out of her skin each time they'd brush against each other––fingers grazing on the bread basket, his sharp intake of breath when she'd turned at an angle to answer the waiter's question and her hair skimmed against his face. Maybe Rafael Cruz had a lot more depth beneath his polished easy-going exterior than she'd given him credit for.

Which made the unwilling attraction she'd held for him since graduate school rise to the surface. But their boss had ordered them to act like they enjoyed each other's company and maybe it was a revelation just how much she liked him. She studied his handsome profile, admiring the strong line of his nose, the carved-from-granite jawline, and those kissable lips. She'd wager her year-end bonus that he knew how to use that mouth.

Phoebe crossed her legs and drew in a deep breath. She couldn't afford to soften her defenses where he was concerned. At the end of the day, she didn't have the band-width for emotional entanglements, especially not with a man who was her career competition. But the temptation to explore her attraction to him was undeniable.

RAFE'S SKIN heated from Phoebe's intense gaze, but he continued talking to Ella about the almost legendary enormous waves she and her husband had seen in Nazaré, Portugal. Sitting next to Phoebe had been exquisite torture. Ice Queen was gone and in her place was a fascinating, witty, interesting woman. He'd never seen this side of her——and yes it was his own damn fault for judging her unfairly——but, damn. She effortlessly volleyed questions with the clients and if he'd met her tonight for the first time, he'd never believe she had a cold bone in that smoking hot body of hers. He'd been rock hard most of the night, on the brink of taking a bite of her creamy bare shoulder.

From her delicate floral scent assaulting his nostrils, to the moment she'd tossed that wild mane of hair against him, to the surprisingly adorable hint of emerging Southern accent as she consumed more wine, she was driving him nuts. If someone had told him he'd find Ms. Hollingsworth cute and funny and sexy, he would have coughed up a lung laughing.

And somehow throughout the endless courses and wine, the scarlet stain of her lipstick remained in place. Which caused his imagination to short-circuit considering what activity would wipe it off. He checked his watch. The charity's chairman was scheduled to speak in an hour and then they'd wrap up the evening. Although Cliff had scheduled a limo to drive them home at 11:00, the visual of sliding into a dark leather backseat with her was a little too appealing. He needed to get it together before then——tonight was about business, not seduction. And definitely not about seduction and Phoebe in the same breath.

He needed some air.

He thrust back from the table and stood. Between the heavy meal and rich desserts and the tease of this now intriguing woman, he needed to cool off before he did something stupid.

Like stroke a hand up her silky thigh to see if her ivory skin was as soft as it looked. Because of course her cut up-to-there slit was on the shapely leg mere inches from his own. Too much temptation.

She angled her head up toward him in surprise. "Are you okay?"

Well, maybe he'd moved a little abruptly. "Fine. I'm just going to grab some air. I'll be back in a few minutes."

One brow winged up in a now familiar gesture and she rose and turned to smile at the table. "We'll be right back, everyone. Don't have too much fun without us."

He retreated a few steps. "What are you doing?" A hint of panic snaked down his spine.

She smiled and looped an arm through his, leading them away from the table. "Don't act weird. Tonight's been going great. We've both had a lot to drink and I could use a few gulps of fresh air myself and we can compare notes." Her accent was definitely a Southern drawl now and she was too damn close to him.

"Compare notes about what?" He made the mistake of tilting his head down and caught another whiff of heavenly scent from that tempting mane of hair.

"About the prospects, silly. What did you think?" Her eyes widened.

He shook his head. His brain urged him to run, but the sensation of her long slender fingers wrapped around his forearm superseded pesky logic. Damn it.

They avoided the crowded terrace patio and stepped into the relative calm of the hallway. But it was December, after all, and Phoebe was in a strapless gown, so seeking another of Rancho Valencia's many open-air spaces wasn't an option. Although right about now he needed a dip in a Nordic Fjord to douse this over-the-top reaction.

His feet kept marching. "The Wine Cave isn't reserved tonight, so we can step in there and catch a few moments of quiet." *What are you doing Cruz? The Wine Cave is dark and secluded. Like the limousine's back seat.*

The massive mahogany wood doors stood ajar, but the brick-lined wine room was empty. Perfect. *Dangerous.*

Phoebe released his arm and strolled into the spectacular private space, those sexy heels echoing along the wooden floors. Reserve wines were showcased in glass cases framing each wall, with ancient oak barrels beneath. The modern chandelier over the long dining table filled the room with an ambient glow. She continued to the back of the room and paused in front of a large mirror which was flanked by two black leather wingback chairs. She shook her titian mane away from her face and leaned closer to stroke her thumb along her plump lower lip.

Rafe sucked in a breath, hauled the doors shut, and stalked to where she stood with her back to him. He stopped mere inches behind her and together they stared at their reflection in the mirror. Those rosy lips parted, her eyes were wide behind her glasses, and the pulse at the base of her neck fluttered against her delicate ivory skin.

Unable to resist any longer, he wrapped one arm around her narrow waist and pulled her back so every inch of her slender back and firm ass plastered against him. She gasped when he splayed his hand across her abdomen and tugged her closer, leaving her no illusion to just how turned on he was. Their eyes remained locked in the mirror and still she remained silent, the only sound in the room their shared heavy breathing. He slid his other hand up to her soft throat and tilted her ivory-skinned neck to one side.

Keeping his gaze locked with hers, he bent his head and raked his teeth against the spot where her neck and shoulder met. Goosebumps erupted on her silky skin, she moaned his name, and her head dropped back against his chest.

Like a splash of fuel, every flaming impulse in him ignited. He dragged her back from the mirror, spun her around, and together they tumbled into one of the wingback chairs. He adjusted her hips on his lap and clasped her face, crushing his mouth against hers. She pressed in closer to him, her lips parting and her sweet tongue wound against his. He slanted his mouth against hers, seeking more. She tasted like heaven and this time he groaned her name.

Her cool hands stroked down his shoulders, exploring, heating his blood with her touch. He released her mouth and his lips traveled across her impossibly soft skin, brushing across her collarbone and nibbling along her shoulder.

"Rafael." She arched her back and breathed his name, her voice huskier now.

Hell even her use of his full name turned him on. "What do you want, beautiful?"

Her breath hitched. "You want me to say it?"

The ridge of his erection strained against his slacks. Hell yes, he wanted her to tell him.

She whispered, "I want you to touch me."

He growled low in his throat. "Touch you where?"

She hissed out a breath and a rosy flush rose up her chest to her high cheekbones. She grabbed his hand and pulled it to her center. "Please. You're driving me crazy."

She was burning hot, even through the silk of her dress. He picked her up and placed her feet on the floor and growled, "Pull your dress up around your waist."

Her eyes narrowed for a moment and she caught her lower lip in her white teeth. She reached for the edges of her long skirt and lifted it up, inch by agonizing inch, and revealed perfect shapely legs. Her eyes gleamed silver and she paused for a moment, holding the skirt's bottom just in front of her sweet core. "I have a little surprise for you."

"Show me." Rafe's hands gripped his hands on his thighs, willing her to hurry up before he lost control and pounced. His heart thundered like he was running a marathon and his jaw clenched.

She raised the scarlet fabric up to her waist revealing that she was bare beneath her gown. That she'd been sitting next to him for hours with no barrier. That he could have reached his hand over underneath the tablecloth and slid his hand up to her thigh. Could have cupped her. Slid a finger inside her. He snapped.

"On my lap now. Spread your legs and sit facing away from me." He bit out each word.

She exhaled, then stepped up to him, turned away and lowered her exquisite body onto his. She arched her back, rocked her hips against his erection, and dropped her head back against him. "Bite my neck again. Then I want your hands all over me."

Holy shit. This was no Ice Queen. This was a powerful woman who knew how to ask for exactly what she wanted. Just like he did. "All you had to do was ask." He lowered his head, pressed his mouth against her throat, and bit down hard enough for her to squirm again. "Too hard?"

"No. Touch me, Rafael." She caught one of his wrists and guided his hand where she wanted it.

He caught her hips in both hands and slowly slid his hands inward and wrapped his fingers around her taut thighs, spreading her legs even wider. Holding her in place with one hand, he cupped her, stroking one finger along her soft folds.

"You're so wet. Is this all for me?" Rafe murmured along her throat, struggling for self-control when all he wanted to do was bury himself inside her now.

"Mmm-hmm. You've been driving me crazy all night."

Her honesty jolted him up another notch. "Me too. You're incredible. Now hold onto the chair." And sexy. And fucking hot as hell.

He started playing with her, stroking, finding her sensitive spots, savoring her moans and the way she worked herself against his hand. Her body started vibrating and he increased his efforts, desperate to feel her come apart on top of him. To give her pleasure.

"Oh my god. Oh my god, yes. Rafael." She cried out, her hips bucking against his hand. He held her tighter against him as wave after wave pulsed through her.

After a few moments, she relaxed back against his torso, and angled her head toward him, her eyes hooded. He slanted his mouth across hers and this time their tongues tangled in a slow, lazy rhythm. She slid one hand up and caught the back of his head, her slender fingers digging into his hair. A surge of unfamiliar possessiveness rose inside him.

"I think it's your turn now." She whispered against his mouth. Then, she swung one graceful leg over and stood, smoothing her dress back down into place.

"My turn?" So why was she dressed again? He wanted to be inside her.

She slid back onto his lap and stroked one hand down his torso, leaving a trail of fire in its wake. She reached the waistband of his pants and paused, gazing up into his eyes. Without a word, she unbuckled his belt and started to slide his zipper down.

He held his breath, his pulse thundering through his veins––mesmerized by the feather-light touch of her fingers. Then she freed him from his pants and wrapped her cool hand around him and he bowed up from the chair. He groaned when she began to caress and grip him tighter.

His breath hissed out and he fisted a hand in her hair, tugging her head back to capture her mouth. Pleasure surged through him. The weight of her against him, the sweet heat of her mouth, the way she seemed to know to touch him exactly how he loved it. Damn.

"Excuse me?" Someone cleared their throat.

Phoebe jumped and they both turned their heads toward the timid voice. *Oh shit.*

"Umm…I'm sorry to bother you, but I'm supposed to close up the wine cave."

Rafe kept Phoebe firmly in his lap with her head turned away from a red-faced, mortified young man in the doorway. "Of course. Can you give us a minute, please? We'll be right out." His voice sounded strained in his own ears.

Another throat clearing cough. "I'll come back in a few minutes. I'm so sorry." The boy turned and fled, slamming the door behind him.

Phoebe leapt up from the chair and ran to the mirror. "Crap, crap, crap. Oh my god, what are we doing?" She smoothed down her dress, fiddled with her glasses, and shook back her mane from her face.

She turned to look at him, her cheeks flaming and her lips swollen.

"It was just one of the staff. Don't worry. You have to admit it's kind of funny. Like we're teenagers getting busted making out in the backseat." Rafe stood and zipped up his fly.

Despite the interruption, he felt pretty damned happy with the world. He had dreaded tonight because he'd assumed Phoebe would be a pain in the ass, but instead she was smart, sarcastic, and sexy. Different from the women he usually spent time with, and he liked her--really liked her. Phoebe was extraordinary and it was less than two hours until the limousine arrived and they could continue this most unexpected and hot evening. He couldn't wait to get her into his bed.

Or go to hers.

He wasn't picky. He just wanted more of the sexy Ms. Hollingsworth who proved all those clichés about still waters running deep were true.

She whirled toward him, her pale hands that had just been perfectly wrapped around him clenched into fists. "Are you out of your mind? There is absolutely not one funny thing about this. This could have been a complete disaster."

Rafe struggled to keep up. "A disaster? I'd say this has been more of a revelation. And once we get back to my place, I'd say tonight would be more of a Christmas miracle." He grinned and stepped toward her.

Her hands flew up in front of her and she jumped back. "A Christmas miracle? You are out of your mind. Tonight was supposed to be when we landed the new clients, remember? And of course you wouldn't worry about your reputation being compromised because it doesn't matter because you're a man." She shook her head, her lips twisting into a frown. "You don't even get how tough it is for women in this industry."

Rafe froze. "Just wait a damn minute. We haven't done a thing except charm everyone at our table. Nobody knows about this. Is this why you act like such a damn nun at work? Because you're worried about your reputation? News alert. It's the 21st century and you can be successful in your career and also have a personal life."

"Well, charm has gotten you far. I can't believe I fell for it. And it's different for women, we have to be perfect and above reproach to succeed." Her full lips compressed into a tight line.

Anger rose in his chest. "So Ms. Hollingsworth is back. You sure know how to flash hot and cold, don't you? Don't put this all on me––you were the one who followed me from the table when I needed a few minutes alone."

She huffed out a breath. "I just wanted––"

A loud cough alerted them that the staff person had returned. *Great. The kid was probably terrified they'd break one of the fancy chairs.*

He squared his shoulders and turned toward the door. "Let's get back to the table. Keep up your end of the bargain tonight. I don't need you blaming me if we don't seal the deal."

Her lips parted like she wanted to say more, but it was too late. He should have known better with her. An unfamiliar feeling of disappointment shot through him but he shook it off.

Showtime.

CHAPTER 4

Phoebe smoothed down her skirt on the silent march back to the ballroom. What the *hell* had just happened? And how could she ever look at a black leather wingback chair again without remembering just *what the hell happened* in the wine cave with Rafael.

What if one of their clients had wandered in looking for them and found her straddling her colleague with her dress up around her waist? *Oh hey, Ella and Mike, give us a moment so Rafael can orgasm too. We work really closely over at Trident.*

She exhaled an unsteady breath. *Pull it together, girl.* She'd worked her tail off since junior high school to build her prestigious career and in one reckless moment she could have jeopardized her reputation as a levelheaded businesswoman. She side-eyed Rafael, who stalked like a panther along next to her, his jaw tight and his hair mussed.

Not that he would suffer the same consequences. Although to be fair, Mr. MacDonald probably had not anticipated them jumping from competitive co-workers to steamy sex partners.

Neither had she.

But Rafael had seemed confident their extreme PDA was a prelude to a one-night stand tonight. Another notch in his bedpost. Granted, she'd been right there along with him, aroused beyond measure by his bossiness and take-charge hands and mouth. A burst of heat pooled in her belly––like a mind-blowing orgasm flashback. No doubt, the next step would have been him bending her over the black leather chair if they hadn't been interrupted.

She could admit that much to herself. Just as she admitted she'd fantasized about him back in graduate school, and well maybe once or twice since she'd joined the firm. The reality of Rafael Cruz blew her sensual daydreams out of the water. Their chemistry was combustible, but purely physical. Right?

She could shield herself against animal attraction, but his obvious love for his family, his agile mind, and genuine niceness had taken her by surprise. Created a chink in her armor against him. During dinner, her protective shell had slipped.

Time to tuck away every single emotion into her impenetrable vault and reinforce her defenses. Rafael had accused of her being able to flip from hot to cold in the blink of an eye. He wasn't wrong. One thing she'd learned in her cutthroat career was to always compartmentalize everything not needed in the present moment. Professional and personal.

Because she was the same as every woman he'd hooked up with––a temporary physical fling that meant absolutely nothing. And she'd seen some of the women he'd been photographed with and although she was confident, she'd never be able to compete with the petite curvy beach babes he seemed to favor. Not that she wanted to compete to become the next flavor of the month. Not that she'd ever once hoped he'd notice her back in graduate school or at the firm.

Nope, not her.

Her pleasant wine buzz had dissolved, a staccato beat

thumping in her temples replacing it. Talk about a major wake-up call. She drew up to her full height and dug into her usually bottomless well of composure. Time to finish out the evening strong.

Nobody would ever suspect what just happened between her and Rafael.

No way would she allow her guard to slip around Rafael Cruz again.

At the entrance to the bustling ballroom, Phoebe caught Rafael's arm, and attempted to ignore the immediate sparks dancing up her skin. "The speaker starts in a few minutes, so we should be good. If everyone wants to chat afterwards, let's move into our divide and conquer strategy with the Samuels and the Levines."

He flicked his dark gaze at her, his warm chocolate eyes frozen into obsidian chips. "Perfect. And don't forget to turn on your warm switch again so the clients don't get frozen out too."

She rolled her eyes and softened her jaw, which yes, she had been gritting her teeth. "Ha ha. You're so funny. Nothing is different––that's crystal clear. Let's do this."

They sauntered back to the table together, two colleagues enjoying a holiday soiree.

"There you two are––what were you up to? We were beginning to worry you'd snuck off to kiss under the mistletoe." Mr. Harmon winked at them from across the table.

Phoebe's breath caught in her throat. "Not exactly. We just needed to..." She paused and swallowed away the bitter taste in her mouth, "clarify a few business matters."

"Uh-oh, all work and no play. Cliff better watch out or you two will be running the firm." Mr. Blake toasted them with his wineglass. "They brought around some excellent port, you should call the server over to make sure you get to try it."

Rafael and Phoebe answered simultaneously. "Not for me."

Phoebe's gaze flicked toward Rafael, who continued to smile at their guests and ignore her, despite their joint unplanned response. So, he also didn't want to risk another sip of inhibition-lowering alcohol either.

Her belly twisted. Although Mr. Harmon's comment was joking, her swollen lips and scattered emotions were real. If they only knew.

Please never let anyone find out.

They both sat down. Earlier the space between them had felt electrically charged. Heated. Now, an icy wall of reserve divided them, as solid as the brick-lined wall of the wine cave. Fine. It was better this way.

She turned her attention to Sasha. Time to revert back to her comfort zone––business mode. Although all she wanted to do was run home and crawl into her bed and bury her head under a pillow or ten. She had the attention span of a hummingbird right now and somehow her usual ease in making conversation had evaporated. Every syllable was a struggle.

In a stroke of fortuitous timing, the charity's chairman stepped onto the stage and tapped the microphone. Phoebe sighed in relief. Now she could simply sit here and listen to the speech and stories of hope and healing and stop being worried about her self-induced problems.

There were people at the event tonight who had lost loved ones or battled this terrible disease and that was what the Jingle Ball was truly about. Raising money for a cure and honoring those lost and bolstering up those in the fight. Her petty issues about securing a new client or getting half-naked with her player co-worker needed to move to the backseat. She'd do well to remember that.

~

RAFE FOUGHT to tune out the fresh scent of her hair. She'd tossed her silky curls over one shoulder and angled her body toward the stage once the speakers began. Although her Ice Queen persona was back, just as he should have known before the fluke in the wine cave, he couldn't seem to ignore her now. Damn it. She shifted again in her seat and—*oh shit*—she had a big fat strawberry of a hickey at the base of her throat. He shifted in his seat at the visceral reminder of just how delectable she'd tasted.

But if he could see the distinctive mark leaping off her pale creamy skin, that meant everyone else could too. She'd flip out if he tried to move her hair to cover the evidence of their tryst, but he had to do something. She'd never forgive him if one of the clients noticed and she'd made a good point—finance *was* a boys' club. He'd never forgive himself if he didn't try to protect her hard-earned reputation.

He casually sipped his water and checked to ensure the rest of the table's focus was on the speaker. He'd be discreet. He lightly tapped her with his elbow to get her attention. She jumped in her seat, apparently not as composed as she looked. She tilted her head toward him and shushed him, her arctic gray eyes narrowed. He held up a finger before she turned her back on him again.

He leaned in and whispered, "Adjust your hair to cover your neck. Act natural."

She sucked in a breath and her eyes widened. "What?"

"Move your hair forward and keep it there. Trust me." Why couldn't she just do as he asked? She'd been eager enough to follow his directions earlier.

And damn it, just seeing her lips swollen from his kisses, and the mark he'd given her and bam—he was rock hard again. She was so close and now he was painfully aware she wore nothing underneath her gown. The memory of her passionate response was too recent. The temptation to see if she'd react the same way again taunted his self-control despite her icy demeanor.

Time to start reciting mathematical formulas in his head, like he'd done as a teenager. What was it about this frustrating woman that challenged his self-control? Most of the women he dated were attractive and successful, but he'd never experienced surges of possessiveness or protectiveness like he had in just a few hours with Phoebe. Learning they both had been the first in their families to pursue ivy league educations, had both busted their butts to earn and maintain scholarships, and were both on equal footing at the firm made the physical chemistry more powerful. Taking the time to unravel Phoebe Hollingsworth's many layers would be like painstakingly unwrapping a highly anticipated Christmas present.

She shifted back in her chair and reached down to the floor to pick up her purse, which of course was close to his foot. Her wild mass of curls skimmed against his thigh and he ground his molars together and held his breath. First, she pursed those full lips and reapplied her scarlet lipstick and it took every ounce of his control not to watch that wand caress her mouth.

Then, she fluffed her hair and readjusted it, so it fell like a cloak of gilded copper ringlets around her bare shoulders. Everything about her beckoned for his touch, but then she peeked back at him, one auburn brow arched. One-hundred percent haughty Ice Queen expression in place.

He nodded and scooted to the far side of his chair, as far from her as possible without falling off the edge.

Her coldness should be enough to douse the heat she stoked in him, damn it. This evening, he'd been charmed and attracted to a warm beautiful brilliant woman who could give as good as she got. And holy hell, their chemistry was like nothing he'd experienced before.

But she'd made it clear that she could turn it on and off like a faucet. Why had she been surprised he'd assumed they'd finish what they started tonight? They'd both been into each other and they were both single, consenting adults. She took compartmentalizing to a whole new level. How was he supposed to keep up?

Whatever. This was why he kept his dating life simple and casual. After the speaker finished, they'd wrap up with the clients and the evening would be finished. And then it would be good riddance Ms. Hollingsworth.

If only they didn't have to share the limo home.

CHAPTER 5

Phoebe stared out of the limousine's long window into the blackness of the winter night. Rancho Santa Fe's winding roads were lined by trees and hedges, the sprawling estates set far back from the road, without many streetlamps. She studiously ignored Rafael's presence, which wasn't difficult because he sat on the other end of the ten-passenger vehicle. She should have just taken an Uber like she had on the way to the event, but no need to alert Cliff to any issues between them.

Nope, just act like the night had been a huge success and not an earth-shattering disaster.

In terms of their business purpose of building connections with the prospects, it had been a resounding triumph. In fact, right now, instead of huddling against the window, she should be sipping some of the excellent champagne resting unopened next to two crystal flutes. Not one, but both of the couples the Harmons had invited this evening had all but assured her and Rafael that they would be coming on board as clients. They'd promised to set up appointments first thing Monday to visit the office and sign on the dotted line.

So why was Phoebe's brain whirring in a ceaseless loop of the wine cave encounter? From the visual of standing together in front of the mirror with his strong square-palmed hand spread across her belly to the soul shattering orgasm on his lap and back again. Where was her compartmentalizing talent when she needed it most? Maybe it had simply flip-flopped because she was trapped in her mind's vault with images of Rafael's mouth on her skin, his hands bringing her pleasure, and the thrill of his bossy commands. Why did she have to have mind-blowing, romance-novel-worthy chemistry with him of all people?

For the rest of her career at Trident Wealth, she'd have to work with him with tonight's episode imprinted in her body and heart. Would she be able to do it?

At least she had the holidays to gather her composure. She'd meet her girlfriend Kimberly to thrash out her frustrations on the tennis court and catch up on client files since she'd left work earlier than usual today. Career had always been her happy place, where she excelled and received recognition for her hard work. How difficult could it be to settle right back in like nothing had happened?

Maybe tonight was a wake-up call and she'd finally set up a dating profile because apparently, she really was in a sexual drought. The one year and one month and four days since she'd last had sex were the primary culprit in her over-the-top response to Rafael. She just needed to get laid and he'd been the man to remind her. *Keep telling yourself that, Phoebe.*

"Earth to Phoebe." Rafael's voice was husky in the shadowed interior of the limo.

She exhaled an unsteady breath. They had to be almost to La Jolla, right? She could handle herself for a few minutes longer.

Her eyes firmly glued to the window, she said, "What is it?"

Rafael sighed. "Will you at least look at me?"

She turned her head and instantly realized her mistake. He'd loosened his tie, exposing his tanned throat where he'd unfastened the top two buttons of his crisp white shirt. If he weren't so damn handsome, this entire debacle would be easier. Well, if he weren't so damn handsome, she'd likely not be in this awkward position. She interlaced her fingers in her lap and raised a brow in question.

He stared at her, his dark eyes gleaming, before he spoke. "Look, I think we should talk about what happened tonight. We're almost to my house, so why don't you come in and we can get everything straightened out before we're back in the office Monday."

She squeezed her hands together. "There's nothing to discuss."

He sighed. "I disagree. Everything's different after tonight and we should talk about it like adults."

She cocked her head and stared at him. "Tonight was a mistake. We just forget it. It never happened. We got the clients, Cliff will be thrilled, and that's it."

His brows drew together. "Look, I don't think what happened is nothing and you're not like the other women––"

She huffed out her breath. "That's right. I'm not like all the casual hook-ups you specialize in. I am not looking to hook-up. There. We've had our discussion. Feel better now?"

He shook his head. "I know you aren't looking for a casual hook-up and neither was I. But you and I––"

Why couldn't he drop it? Why was her heart pounding against her ribs? "There is no you and I. Look, you're a guy, you should be thrilled I'm making this easy for you. We had a hot moment, but for a million reasons, it cannot happen again. We'll simply ignore each other at the office, which has worked well so far. So there's nothing to discuss and no reason for me to come inside your house. Got it?"

His eyes cooled and he shifted back against the smooth burgundy leather seat. "Sorry I asked. Don't worry, I won't make that mistake twice."

The limo pulled to a stop. "And here's my house. Enjoy the rest of your evening, Ms. Hollingsworth." With that parting quip, he yanked open the door and closed it quietly behind him.

Phoebe pulled off her glasses and pinched the bridge of her nose. She didn't understand what he was trying to do. They really didn't have to talk about being professional in the office. They'd landed the clients and their boss would be thrilled and there wasn't any additional competition between them. And so there was no need to rehash tonight. Ever.

Truth be told, she didn't trust herself to be alone with him again. The bottom line was she wanted him more than she'd ever wanted any man before. And her crush-from-afar at school was no longer a distant memory now that she'd seen this different side of him. Not just the blazing chemistry but learning he wasn't a superficial jerk like she'd assumed. In fact, he was the total package, and didn't that just make it all worse. Talking herself out of her physical attraction was one thing because she'd assumed he was a man slut.

Now that maybe he was a good guy who, like her, worked hard and didn't have time for a serious relationship or hadn't met the right person either? They were both thirty-three years old and single. And obviously they'd each held deep-seated erroneous judgments about each other.

Tonight, she'd allowed him to see beyond her "all business all the time" mask. Allowed herself to be vulnerable with him. And then she'd totally shut him down when he'd suggested they talk like adults. Because she was afraid of being alone with him and losing control again. So who was acting shallow now? And immature.

Phoebe straightened up in her seat. She didn't want to be this kind of person. A person governed by fear of rejection or fear of abandonment after one night. She liked and respected the Rafael she'd seen tonight, the man beneath the charm. And why wouldn't he assume they'd pick up where they left off tonight? It wasn't like she would have stopped him if they hadn't been interrupted. She wanted him.

They did need to talk and handle this situation like grown-ups. She snatched up her purse and fished out her phone. She'd text him and invite him to have coffee in the morning and go from there. At the very least, they could be friendly toward each other. There was no reason to act like he was her nemesis.

She'd always pursued what she wanted in every other area of her life and now she wanted Rafael. Or at least to see if there was more to them than that incredible physical connection and snarky banter.

Before she could start typing, a message from Rafe popped up.

I respect you didn't want to come in tonight. I still want to talk. Meet me at Brick and Bell at 10 tomorrow?

Phoebe stared at the text for a moment—okay, she'd been about to ask him to meet her at her favorite coffee place, Brick and Bell in downtown La Jolla. Uncanny. She started to reply then stopped. Squared her shoulders.

What did she want? To toss and turn all night and replay the evening or go for what she wanted? At this point, she couldn't tell if she and Rafael were meant to be together or if maybe they were simply meant to hook up. But if she allowed this window of opportunity to slip away now because she didn't know the answer, she'd be a fool.

She dropped the phone onto the seat next to her and

scooted forward to knock on the panel separating her from the driver. When the opaque screen slid noiselessly down, he glanced back. "What can I do for you, miss?"

"Could you please turn the limo around and take me back to Mr. Cruz's place?"

He nodded, his expression revealing nothing. "Of course. We'll be back there in no time."

"Thank you." She lifted the divider again and gazed around the luxurious limo they'd wasted on the way home. If Rafe were half as talented on a long stretch of leather seat as he was standing or perched on an armchair…Heat rose in her cheeks.

She pulled out her compact and lipstick from her purse, reapplied her scarlet pout, and skimmed her hair away from her flushed face. Nerves fluttered along her skin and her pulse thrummed in her temples and throat. Anxiety notwithstanding, she'd see Rafe, have a grown-up discussion with him, and whatever happened, happened.

The limo purred to a halt. Phoebe blew out a breath. Showtime. The gleam from the champagne bottle caught her eye. May as well bring it inside since they hadn't celebrated yet. If nothing else, they could toast to landing two new major clients for the firm.

But if she had her way, she'd take charge this time and Rafael wouldn't know what hit him. And if he wanted to boss her around a little bit, who was she to stop him?

CHAPTER 6

$\mathcal{P}$hoebe clutched the chilled champagne bottle in one hand and sauntered toward the enormous turquoise front door of Rafe's cream Mediterranean home. The house had beautiful curving lines, a terracotta tiled roof, and clusters of fuchsia bougainvillea. La Jolla shared a lot of similarities to the South of France and Rafe's house perched high on a gently sloping hill on Mt. Soledad didn't disappoint.

Ignoring the trembling in her legs, she took a cleansing breath and knocked. She hadn't even lowered her hand before he whipped open the door. For a moment they simply stared at each other. He'd changed out of his black tie and wore low-slung gray sweats, a faded blue San Diego Padres t-shirt, and thick wool socks. Of course, he looked delicious, even in ancient loungewear.

His dark eyes were wide, but she couldn't read his expression. "You're here."

She nodded and cleared her throat. "Um, I was about to text you back, but I thought it would be better for us to talk in person. Is that okay?"

He stepped back and waved her inside. "Better than okay. And you brought champagne?"

She shrugged a shoulder and smiled sheepishly. "Well, Cliff had it in the limo for us and we did win those clients tonight, so I didn't want it to go to waste."

He closed the door and they paused in the foyer. "I just started a fire in the living room. We can talk in there."

She swallowed the nerves thrumming in her throat. She followed him down the wide hallway that boasted wide-planked honey colored hardwood floors, soaring ceilings, and brightly colored paintings that brought the cream walls alive. Scents of evergreen filled the air when they entered a broad open doorway, a Christmas tree that had to be fifteen feet high sparkled with lights and colorful ornaments.

Floor-to-ceiling windows made up the far wall of the large but surprisingly cozy living room. An enormous caramel-color L-shaped couch and two leather armchairs were set before a tall white-bricked fireplace. Still chilly from the cool San Diego evening air, she crossed to warm her hands in front of the crackling fire. And take a moment to gather her composure.

"Do you want a sweatshirt or should I open the champagne now?" Rafe's words were polite, even careful.

"The fire is just what I needed. I don't know when I'll get used to how cool it gets at night here––the days are so mild." And she really needed to stop babbling about the weather.

"That's the best part of Southern California, warm days and cool nights. Have a seat and I'll grab a few glasses and be right there." Rafe crossed to a wine cabinet against the far wall, popped the champagne, and poured it into a couple flutes.

Phoebe sank into the comfortable sofa and accepted the champagne from Rafael. When their fingers brushed, goosebumps erupted on her upper arms. Again.

Rafe grabbed a velvety soft burgundy throw and tucked it around her shoulders. "There, you're all wrapped up now and won't freeze. So, do you want to go first or should I?"

Although Phoebe's intention had been to charge in and explain why she'd been so harsh, now that she was actually here with him, her nerves were kicking in. She wasn't any good at talking about her feelings––she'd grown up in a loving family, but she'd been one of the guys with her brothers and nobody was particularly demonstrative.

For whatever reason, that hadn't really been an issue before. Granted, her past romantic relationships tended to be short-lived because she'd literally not had the time to get past certain points with most of them. And twice when she'd dated guys she could imagine a future with, they'd wanted her to choose between her career and them.

Career had always won.

Somehow she didn't think Rafael would ever ask her to choose. If it came to that point.

Rafe's lips quirked. "How about a toast first. Then I'll start." He leaned forward and clinked his glass against hers. "To a productive business event and interesting developments."

Phoebe relaxed and sipped the spectacular drink. "Look, Rafael, I appreciate you texting me, but let me start, please. And I agree on the business and the…umm…developments. So, I tend to be more successful at work than in my personal life. I don't know how you manage to do both."

Rafe shook his head. "If you could talk to my brother and sister-in-law, they would assure you I definitely am not successful in my personal life. I know you think I'm a player and yeah, I've dated a lot of women. But work has always been my number one priority and it was just easier to keep things on a casual level. I think my longest relationship was in college and that was about a year."

Phoebe nodded. "Same for me. College was easier, because, well, I was twenty. The pressure to be on top doesn't leave a lot of energy for much else. And grad school..." A vision of drooling over Rafael from afar popped up and her cheeks warmed.

Rafe cocked his head. "And grad school?"

Damn it. She'd lay it on the line. "Well, I had a crush on someone who didn't know I existed, so I buried myself in work. And then--"

Rafe held up a hand. "Whoa whoa whoa. A crush on someone?"

Phoebe ran her tongue around her teeth. Now or never. "You. I had a crush on you. And you never noticed. When coincidence or fate or whatever had Cliff recruit me for Trident, I almost turned him down because you were there. But it was the opportunity of a lifetime and I took it."

Rafael rubbed his hand along his jaw. "I had no idea."

"All it took for you to notice is me wearing my hair down." She smiled wryly. "But, let me finish. I was ready to leave the east coast. None of my relationships lasted longer than three or four months." She exhaled and sipped her champagne.

"Yeah, I think my longest has been about the same. We're on the quarter system. So we're really actually alike, but I've just been more public."

She nodded. "And that's part of why I freaked out tonight. I've made assumptions about you because of all the women, and I realize that isn't really fair. As a female, especially in our industry where I'm one of a few, I can't afford to have anyone make assumptions. In this day and age, there shouldn't be a double standard, but there is. And it stinks. So I'm sorry for how I spoke to you tonight. I freaked out. I wasn't expecting to like you so much and I definitely wasn't expecting what happened..."

He flashed a wicked grin. "I don't think either of us expected what happened to happen." He reached one hand out and brushed her hair back over her shoulders. "And I'm sorry about the hickey."

Phoebe laughed even though her heartbeat accelerated, and heat spread down to her center from his gentle touch. "I cannot believe I have my first hickey at thirty-three years old."

His eyes widened. "Your first? Lucky me. Can I say a few things now?"

She nodded.

He reached for her hand and intertwined his fingers with hers. "I'm sorry about being an ass at work. I've been there my whole career and Cliff starts raving about this east coast dynamo joining our firm and you arrived and barely spoke to me. I assumed you were a snob and ignored you. Not very professional, but for some reason you got under my skin."

"Is this supposed to be an apology because so far…" She tugged her hand and he held tight.

"I'm sorry I made assumptions about you, and I'm sorry about Harvard. I swear I never saw you before you set foot into Trident's office. But now that we've spent time together, I have to say you are the most fascinating, beautiful, complicated smartass of a woman I've ever met. And I'd figured that out before the wine cave incident." Sincerity shone in his warm whiskey brown eyes.

"The wine cave incident? Is that what we're calling it?" Excitement danced along her skin.

"Yeah, that's what we're calling it. I'd been turned on all night sitting next to you and once I touched you…" His eyes hooded and he leaned closer, the heat from his body singing her bare skin.

She licked her lips. "So now we've both apologized. We both realize our chemistry is off the charts…"

"Yes, our chemistry is intense. But this isn't just sex. I like you, Phoebe Hollingsworth. I'd like to see you again. Outside of work. Will you go out with me?"

And now she was melting inside. "I like you too, Rafael Cruz. I will go out with you." She jerked back. "Wait. What about the promotion?"

"What?" His dark brows drew together.

She placed a hand against his chest. "The only thing we didn't discuss was what happens at the firm next year. We both want to take over, right?"

Damn, he'd forgotten. How wild was that? "I don't think that's something we figure out right now. Is it a game changer for you?"

"I mean, it's a big reason I moved to San Diego. But Cliff probably isn't going anywhere for the next year, right? So we have time to figure it all out." Her fingers curled into his t-shirt, pulling him closer. "I do think we should double check to make sure that the wine cave incident wasn't a fluke. I'd like you to kiss me please."

Rafe reached forward and gently removed her glasses, placing them down on the table behind the couch. He slid his hands into her hair and tugged her head back, holding her in place. "When you ask so nicely, how could I refuse?" He lowered his head and captured her mouth.

She wove her arms around his neck and swirled her tongue against his, taking the kiss deeper. He shifted and pulled her down with him onto the fluffy patterned rug in front of the crackling fire. His hands roamed all over her body and excitement tingled along her skin, and heat flared in her center.

After a few satisfying moments in his embrace, Phoebe lifted her head. "I'm confident the wine cave incident was no fluke. You?" She ran her hands along his lean muscular frame and began to lift off his shirt, desperate to caress his smooth bronzed skin.

His sculpted mouth skimmed along her skin and he murmured, "Almost. I think to be completely sure we are making a wise investment, we need to get naked. Now."

She arched under his touch. "Mmm-hmm, oh yes, let's be sure. Unzip me."

He growled and his teeth grazed the tender spot on the side of her neck. "Hold still." In a flash, he freed her from the long silky swath of fabric and shoved it down around her waist. He paused, leaned back, and gazed at her, the crackle and pop of the flames the only sound in the room.

"You are so beautiful." He stroked one strong hand down her shoulder, along the sensitive side of her ribcage, and gripped her hip. Goosebumps erupted along her skin, despite the heat from the fireplace behind her.

Her gaze blurred when he trailed his fingers up and captured her breast, stroking his thumb across her taut nipple. He shifted closer and his mouth closed over the sensitive flesh, his tongue stroking and arousing her. Sparks jolted straight to her center and she murmured his name.

He yanked her closer and crushed her against his solid torso. She wrapped her arms around his waist and melted against him. Closer, she couldn't get close enough. His mouth slanted against hers, coaxing her lips apart, his tongue tangling with hers. His warm sweet breath melded with hers and the only thought her brain could form was *more*. She needed more.

She grabbed the hem of his t-shirt and tugged, eager to feel his skin against hers. She raked her nails up his back and he groaned. He shifted away from her and ripped off the shirt, pitching it away. Before he could move, she placed one hand against the satiny skin covering his sculpted pecs and stroked down the carved ridges of his abdominals. He sucked in a harsh breath, but froze in place.

For a moment their eyes locked, his whiskey brown eyes aflame. Without shifting her gaze, she slid her fingers down to the hem of his sweatpants and pressed her palm against his impressive erection.

"We were interrupted earlier tonight." She whispered and reached inside his pants and wrapped her fingers around him. "I think you should come closer."

"Phoebe." He rasped her name.

"Rafael." Her lips curved up, savoring his arousal, the heat flashing off his skin. "I'm dying to find out if you taste as good as you feel."

"Woman, you're going to kill me tonight." In a lightening quick move, he shifted onto his back and she rolled with him.

"No, I'm going to make you feel good tonight." She pressed an open-mouthed kiss on his chest. His small flat nipples hardened as she trailed feather-light kisses along his carved torso.

His breath hissed out and he stroked her hair with one hand, tangling his fingers in her unruly waves. She nibbled and kissed her way along his flat stomach, pausing to pay special attention to the grooved muscle along his hipbones. A dark trail of hair started beneath his navel and disappeared into those sexy sweatpants.

She adjusted her position before gently guiding his sweats off. He lifted his hips and reached with his other hand to shed the barrier between them. His erection sprang free and she wrapped one hand around him and gazed up at him for a split second before licking him from base to tip. He bowed up and his fingers tightened on her scalp.

She smiled against him and used her mouth to drive him crazy, loving every groan as he moved with her.

He wrapped his hand in her hair and gently tugged. "Phoebe, come up here, I need to kiss you."

Taking her time, she made her way up toward his mouth, teasing him with her leisurely pace. He captured her hips and shifted her so she straddled him, her bare thighs framing his hips, his arousal digging into her center. Her evening gown was bunched around her waist, but she didn't care. Every single spot where their flesh touched burned and her breath caught in her throat looking down at him.

He pulled her down and crushed his lips against hers, and desire flamed through her. His hands cupped her ass, holding her against him and she rocked her hips into him, wanting—no—craving more. Now.

He lifted her off him and quickly removed her dress. "I want to feel all of you and that material had to go." He rolled them onto their side and lifted one of her legs and draped it over his hip.

They were face to face and he captured her mouth again, his talented tongue swirling against hers. He slid one hand between them, cupping her. "Oh my god, you're so ready for me, babe." He groaned and thrust one finger inside her, then a second, stroking until he found that spot that made her scream. He pressed his thumb against her, while finding a rhythm that drove her mad. Already aroused, within seconds waves pulsated through her, and she exploded in one light-shimmering climax.

"Rafael, I need you inside me. Now please. Do you have protection?" She murmured against his mouth. If she didn't have him inside her now, she might lose her mind.

He stiffened. "Upstairs. Are you sure?"

She rocked against him again. "Never been more sure in my life." Never wanted anyone the way she desired Rafael and never experienced such intense chemistry. Not a single reason arose to cause her to hesitate. No, she wanted him now.

Before she could take another breath, Rafe rolled to the side and he swept her up into his arms. "Upstairs."

He fused his mouth against hers and strode out of the room and carried her like she was light as a feather. She thrust her fingers into his thick hair and arched against him, heat igniting along every inch of her body. Her heart thundered against her ribcage, her pulse thrumming violently, with each step closer to his bedroom. A cool burst of air blasted her when he laid her down onto an enormous bed before he joined her, bracing his muscular forearms to shield her from his full weight.

"Protection. Now." She managed to utter the words when all she wanted to do was grab his perfect ass and drive every inch of him inside her, precaution be damned.

He growled and bit her lower lip and levered away from her toward the bedside table. Her head dropped to the side, admiring the ripple of sinewy muscles as he delved into a drawer and grabbed a foil packet. He shifted back and paused, gazing down at her. "I want you."

She shivered under the intensity of his dark gaze and reached an arm toward him. "I'm all yours."

He ripped open the packet and rolled on the condom, never breaking the connection of their eyes. Anticipation and impatience danced along her skin as he positioned himself between her legs. Slowly, he settled his weight against her and the moment their skin touched, her entire being liquefied and a moan tore through her.

His pupils dilated and his jaw tightened. He reached one hand up, caressed her cheek, then crushed his lips against hers, plundering her mouth.

Then, he slowly entered her, filling her inch by inch. She

held her breath, working to accommodate him, until they were connected completely.

Her breath whooshed out and she gripped his ass, holding him immobile. "Give me a minute." Holy hell--he was enormous. Gloriously enormous.

He held himself still, slanted his mouth against hers, and kissed her deeply. "Let me know when you're ready. You feel incredible." His voice was gravelly.

"You feel pretty incredible yourself." She sighed, then rocked her hips up against him, ready for more.

They began to move, slowly at first, exploring, and finding a sensual rhythm. Natural. Primal. Hot. Like they'd done this before. Sensation and passion overtook her--until her entire world was them together. She wrapped her legs around his waist and urged him to go deeper, faster, harder. Every stroke enflamed her and the sweet pressure built until another climax blazed through her.

"Oh my god, Phoebe." His hands tightened on her hips as he followed her over the edge. His full weight crushed her for a moment before he enfolded her in his arms and rolled them to one side without breaking their intimate connection.

"Oh my god is right." Her entire body trembled. Phoebe slid her hands up into Rafe's thick hair and tugged his face closer. His lips met hers, his kiss tender now.

He murmured against her mouth, "Give me a second." He withdrew and went to the bathroom she hadn't noticed--how could she have noticed anything but him--and she rolled onto her back again, stretching her arms overhead and savoring the delicious languor in her limbs. She stared at the high ceiling and allowed her heavy eyelids to drift shut. Rafe slid back into the fluffy sheets with her and snuggled her in close, pressing a kiss into her hair. "Sweet dreams, Phoebe."

Her final thought before she allowed sleep to claim her: Wow. Tonight had most definitely not turned out how she'd expected.

CHAPTER 7

Rafe's phone buzzed and he rolled to his side and grabbed it off the nightstand. His firefighter brother Jake's number flashed on the screen with a "Call me ASAP" message. His brother wasn't prone to dramatics, so Rafe leapt out of bed, instantly alert.

Phoebe grumbled, turned over, and dragged a pillow over her wild spill of fiery curls. The sheets slipped, revealing one creamy shoulder. His lips quirked. Not a morning person—he'd need to remember that.

He grabbed his sweats off the floor and headed downstairs. Might as well make some coffee—they hadn't slept much last night. His body reacted to the memories of the living room, and the shower, and his bed. The wine cave incident had most definitely *not* been a fluke. How would he ever get enough of the intriguing icy hot Phoebe Hollingsworth?

If he had his way, the wine cave incident was the beginning of a mutually beneficial merger. A long-term merger.

Once he reached the kitchen, he called Jake. "Everything okay?"

"Yeah, well, I need a favor." Jake rarely asked for help--too damn stubborn--so this was curious.

"Anything." He'd do anything for his brother and his parents.

"Can you call Dad? Amanda's parents invited all of us for Christmas Eve and you know Dad likes to make his famous Christmas Eve dinner. Please." Jake had recently married into the McNeill clan and now lived with them at Pacific Vista Ranch.

Rafe took out the French Roast beans and coffee grinder. "They are so damn happy at least one of their sons is married, I'm sure he and Mom will be fine with it. I'll call and ask him to prepare his feast on Christmas Day instead. On one condition."

"Sure." Jake's deep voice was eager.

"Ask Amanda if I can bring a date."

Jake groaned. "Man, seriously? This is family."

Rafe paused and rubbed his hand across his chest. "I met someone. She's different."

Jake was silent for a few moments. "What's her name and where did you meet her?"

"Phoebe. Her name is Phoebe. She's incredible. Special. We work together."

"Work together? Isn't that asking for trouble if things don't work out? I mean, what if it messes with your promotion?"

His brother knew Rafe had never allowed anyone or anything to affect his career. He shoved aside a flicker of doubt--Phoebe was different. "Look, I want you to meet her and I don't want her to be alone on Christmas. Deal?"

"Deal. My big brother met someone--it's a Christmas miracle. I can't wait to tell Amanda she doesn't have to meet another of your flavors-of-the-week." Jake laughed.

Jake rolled his eyes. "Come on, I'm not that bad."

Jake snorted and continued to chuckle.

"Hey, do you want me to call Dad or not?" His brother could stop laughing anytime.

"Sorry. Seriously, I want to meet her if you like her this much. Thanks for working your magic on Dad. And are you bringing her to our parents' house on Christmas Day too?" Jake asked.

"Yeah. Thanks and see you Thursday." Rafe turned to close the kitchen door before hitting the coffee grinder and froze.

Phoebe stood in the doorway, looking disheveled and adorable in one of his old Harvard sweatshirts. "I'm incredible and you're making plans for Christmas?" She squinted at him and he realized when he'd carried her upstairs last night, she'd left her glasses in the living room.

He crossed the room in three strides, wrapped her in his arms, and set her on the granite countertop. He stepped between her legs and stroked his hands up her smooth firm thighs. "Well, I was going to come upstairs and bring you coffee and convince you to stay in bed with me all morning. I think you're incredible. But since you heard me, yeah I'd like you to spend Christmas with me."

She bit her full lower lip, bare and pink this morning, "Oh, I'm already convinced about staying in bed. But Christmas with family is a big deal…"

Rafe gently brushed her hair away from her face. "Phoebe, I've never brought a woman to Christmas before. I know it's fast, but I meant it when I said I wanted us to see where we could take this."

Her eyebrows drew together. "And you're not concerned about what happens when we return to the office?"

"We're two intelligent people who can handle keeping our professional and personal lives separate." *At least up until last night.* He captured her delicate ivory face between his hands and pressed his mouth against her soft lips, delving into her warm, sweet kiss.

He tilted his head back and met her wide pewter gaze. "And I feel like we really met for the first time at the Jingle Ball. Kind of like an unexpected gift. My family means the world to me and the McNeills live on this incredible ranch in Rancho Santa Fe. You'll love it."

"I can't believe this is happening. I've always made it home for the holidays, so this year was going to be tough without my family." She smiled and ran her fingers down his chest. "Yes, I'd love to spend Christmas with you."

Heat rose beneath the light scrape of her fingernails and every muscle in his body tightened. He slanted his mouth over hers. "In the meanwhile, I've got a few ideas for this morning."

She slid her hands into his hair and murmured against his lips. "Oh really? I don't have to be at work for about a week."

He shifted back, whipped off the sweatshirt, and ran his hands down her gorgeous naked body. "What a coincidence, Ms. Hollingsworth. Neither do I."

"Merry early Christmas to us." Her lips curved up and she pulled his head down to meet her kiss.

CHAPTER 8

*P*hoebe drank in the rolling verdant pastures, dense clusters of trees, and boundless blue sky from the passenger seat of Rafe's black BMW, her lips parted in awe. Once they'd crossed through the towering guarded gate into Pacific Vista Ranch, the real world receded and an enchanting fairy tale land emerged, sprawled over the two hundred plus acre horse breeding ranch. Heck, the line between reality and fantasy seemed to merge with each beautiful day and romantic night she'd spent with Rafe.

He parked next to a few cars lined up in front of a sprawling cream-colored Mediterranean-style estate, flicked off the engine, and reached over and pressed his broad hand over her clasped ones. Phoebe stared up at the enormous gleaming windows and explosion of vibrant flowers framing the home's grand entryway.

"Pretty amazing, right? The first time I came here with Jake, I was blown away." He leaned in and nuzzled her cheek.

Sparks tingled down her spine. "I just can't imagine living somewhere like this. I mean--wow."

"Chris McNeill was one of the top dogs in Hollywood for

decades before buying the property. Now Jake's sister-in-law Sam has turned the breeding operation into one of the most successful in the country. Even though they're wealthy, they earned it, and they are really down-to-earth. You aren't nervous to meet them?" He angled his head back and raised one dark brow.

"Not the McNeills. Maybe a little nervous about meeting your parents."

She released an unsteady exhale. Toss in a dash of anxiety centered around their romantic whirlwind week. How could she be spending Christmas Eve and Christmas Day with his parents when less than a week ago, she'd assumed he would never be more than her competition and rival? And would their bubble burst when they returned to the office?

"My parents are great--don't worry. My brother hit the jackpot when he married Amanda." Rafe drew her hands up and pressed a warm kiss on her fingers before releasing her and opening his door. "Come on, let's head inside."

Playing well with others was one of her top life skills, so she could handle a holiday celebration with Rafael's family. Phoebe squared her shoulders and stepped out of the car. She grabbed the bottle of Napa Cabernet and festive tin of Belgian chocolates from the backseat and joined Rafe where he stood waiting.

Damn--he was handsome, his dark hair burnished in the winter sunlight, his chiseled lips curved into a welcoming smile. Her heart tumbled in her chest from the warmth shining in his whiskey brown eyes. Fairy tale or real life?

He took the wine and interlaced his long fingers with hers. Together they approached the massive wooden front door, which had to stand twenty feet high. Before Rafe could knock, the door flung open and a willowy blonde and a dark-haired titan greeted them.

The giant enveloped Rafe in a bear hug. "Thank god

you're here. Dad's already pestering Angela in the kitchen and you need to play interference."

The woman laughed and shook her head. "Jake, you're exaggerating. Angela will boot him out if he's bothering her." She extended one slender hand. "You must be Phoebe. I'm Amanda and this guy is my husband, Jake."

Phoebe could only stare for a moment when Jake released Rafe. The resemblance between the brothers was clear, but where Jake looked like he could fell a tree with one brawny arm, Rafe's looked more like the lean panther lounging on one of the tree's branches. Another flutter, this time in her belly. She shifted her gaze and smiled into Amanda's brilliant emerald eyes.

"Nice to meet you. I'm Phoebe. Rafe tells me you're a veterinarian?"

Amanda's lips curved up. "Yes, I'm the resident equine vet. And you work with Rafael?"

Rafe slid his arm around Phoebe's waist and her skin instantly heated beneath her ruby red cashmere sweater. "I do. I moved out here a few months ago from the East Coast."

A brown dog galloped up and bumped into Jake's legs. Rafe's brother reached down and scratched the dog's ears. "Hi Phoebe, I'm Jake and this is Stella, our firstborn."

Phoebe crouched down in front of the dog and laughed when Stella butted against her cheek and swiped her glasses with her big pink tongue. "What a sweetheart. I miss having a pet."

"If you work hours like Rafe does, that doesn't leave a lot of time for a dog, but maybe a couple of cats would work with your schedule." Amanda smiled again.

"I grew up with a menagerie, so one of these days." Phoebe stood, removed her glasses, and wiped them on her charcoal striped silk scarf.

"Well, let's head back." They fell in step with Rafe's

brother and his wife, while Stella bounded down a wide biscuit-colored hallway with high ceilings and polished hardwood floors. Phoebe worked not to gape at the open doorways which showcased floor-to-ceiling windows and oversized furniture, accented by colorful rugs. When they approached what must be the kitchen and dining room, delicious scents filled the air and the volume of raised voices amplified with every step.

Amanda turned to Phoebe. "I know the McNeill clan can seem overwhelming at first, but I promise we don't bite. And the Cruzes are the sweetest couple."

Phoebe returned her smile. Accustomed to being the only daughter with obnoxious older brothers, she could hold her own. But she hadn't met the parents of a guy she'd dated in eons. Nerves simmered beneath her skin. Especially because she and Rafe had only been "dating" for less than a week.

"There they are. Rafael and his beautiful lady." A tall olive-skinned man wearing a Frosty the Snowman apron and a Santa hat hurried over from behind an enormous pale granite island laden with cheerful colored dishes.

Rafe tensed next to Phoebe. "I apologize in advance for my dad." He whispered in her ear, his warm breath causing the small hairs on the back of her neck to stand up at attention. Hadn't he said not to worry?

"So this is the first woman who my son has brought home for Christmas. Phoebe, I can't tell you how thrilled we are to meet you. I'm Eduardo, your future father-in-law." Rafe's dad shook her hand vigorously, his dark eyes gleaming.

Phoebe's mouth fell open.

"Eduardo, stop embarrassing her." A curvy chestnut-haired woman stepped up with a wry grin. "Hi Phoebe, I'm Lisa, Rafael's mom. Please ignore my husband. He specializes in being annoying. Part of his 'artistic temperament.'"

Phoebe recovered enough to speak. "Don't worry, I'm

used to being teased—I've got older brothers. It's lovely to meet you both." Okay, Rafe's mom was charming but his dad was over-the-top.

Identical redheads waved from a large breakfast nook where they sat with two handsome guys sipping cocktails. "Hi Phoebe. I'm Dylan and this is Sam. Our husbands, Gabriel and Holt. Grab a drink and come join us. We're just about to start our annual Monopoly game and you two are officially recruited."

A tall brunette sporting a red "Kiss me I'm the Chef" apron grinned at her. "Nice to meet you Phoebe. I'm Angela. We've got some hors d'œuvres at the end of the island, so feel free to grab a plate and join the game. Watch out, Holt and Sam are really competitive."

"Hey, they're the finance gurus, I'm sure they'll be fine." Sam called out with a chuckle.

Phoebe greeted everyone, her anxiety evaporating. On the far end of the great room, by a massive stone fireplace, what had to be a twelve-foot Christmas tree twinkled with lights and filled the festive atmosphere with the scent of evergreen. Flames from white and gold candles flickered cheerfully, and pots simmered on the enormous gas range. Late afternoon glimmers of sunshine from oversized windows sparkled and danced over the holly-patterned dishes and scarlet napkins adorning an enormous oak table.

"Hi Phoebe. I'm Chris. Merry Christmas. Please win Monopoly so we don't have to hear Samantha sing 'We are the Champions' all year." The McNeill patriarch, a tall, ruggedly handsome man sporting a Santa hat, grinned and shook his head. "We've got an excellent Cabernet open or there are plenty of other choices."

"Let me pour. I know this wine is one of Rafael's favorites. Do you want Cab as well, Phoebe?" Amanda crossed to the makeshift bar area, where an assortment of bottles and holiday-themed glasses waited on the counter by a large stainless-steel refrigerator.

She and Rafe followed Amanda across the room and added the bottle they'd brought to the impressive collection. They certainly wouldn't run out of booze tonight. Or this year, for that matter.

"We have the same taste in wine, don't we?" Rafe smiled and pressed a kiss on the top of Phoebe's hair.

Amanda froze for a moment, her eyes enormous, then quickly recovered. "Two glasses then?"

Heat flooded Phoebe's cheeks. Rafe's casual affection apparently was something new, at least to his sister-in-law. Not that she minded. Hell, she loved each brush of his fingers, touch of his lips, and the ever-present wicked glint in his eye when he looked at her.

Drinks in hand, they slid into the cushioned seats and his brother and Amanda squeezed into the spacious booth with them.

"Okay, Phoebe and Rafe, you get first choice." Holt said, his brilliant blue eyes sparkling. "Just know my wife thinks that the dog is her lucky charm. And I'll be in charge of the bank."

Sam rolled her eyes and elbowed her husband. "As if I need luck. Please. Take the dog if you want."

Phoebe laughed. "I'll take the top hat." Although she hadn't played in years, Monopoly was her favorite board game from childhood. She'd been the Hollingsworth family champion, much to her brothers' chagrin.

"Prepare to surrender your trophy, Sam. I'm going to win this one, sorry." Rafe flashed his cocky grin and plucked up the race car.

"I'm used to playing the version set in Paris, but don't count me out." Gabriel said in his husky French accent and selected the penguin.

Everyone else chose their tokens, Holt dealt the colorful cash, and they settled into passing Go, snapping up real estate, and evading jail. Banter bounced back and forth across the table, and cheerful classic Christmas tunes hummed in the background. Rafe captured Phoebe's hand underneath the table.

Her heart warmed––she was simply happy. Although she couldn't be with her own family this Christmas, the heat of Rafe's powerful thigh against her own, the comfort of an old familiar game with friendly people, and the delicious wine added up to an ideal evening. No need for her to stress about the future. Despite his dad's father-in-law comment.

"Okay, Grant won't be here for another hour or so, let's focus and knock this game out." Amanda glanced at her watch, rolled the dice, and moved her metal cat forward five spaces. "And Holt, hand over four houses, please."

"You guys are always so serious. We can chat and play––it is a game after all. Phoebe, tell us how you and Rafe met." Dylan flicked her long auburn hair over one shoulder.

The wine cave incident flashed before Phoebe's eyes and she jolted, her wine sloshing over the rim of her glass. No way could the McNeills know about their X-rated hook-up. Universe willing that there weren't hidden security cameras at the posh resort.

Rafe quickly wiped up the splash of burgundy liquid from the table. "We work together." He answered, one broad hand squeezing her thigh.

"Well, yes, but that doesn't explain what you're doing *not* working together. So spill it." Dylan's brown eyes lit with mischief. "Details, please."

"Dylan, don't be rude. Sam, it's your turn." Amanda scolded one sister and directed the other. It was clear she was the older sister, used to being in charge.

Dylan's dark brows drew together. "I'm sorry I'm not

trying to be rude, it's just we've known Rafael for a while now and Phoebe's the first normal--" She bit her lip.

Phoebe sat up straighter. "It's okay." She liked that these people saw her as different for Rafael.

"Here's the short version. We both went to Harvard for grad school, but didn't meet each other there. I got an offer I couldn't refuse at Trident Wealth and it just so happened Rafe worked there too. We, umm…didn't really get to know each other until our boss had us attend a charity event together last week and we…" She ran her tongue around her teeth. "hit it off."

And I'm falling for him. She didn't dare look at Rafe because his firm grip on her leg was already upsetting her equilibrium.

Rafe's lips quirked. "What she didn't mention is that up until last week, we had a bit of a rivalry. But now we've seen the error of our ways. I think she's the most incredible woman I've ever met. Even though I'm going to beat her at Monopoly tonight."

Phoebe's heart knocked against her ribs at the same time mirth bubbled up in her throat. He always managed to make her laugh even when he was also offering the most outrageous compliments. Did he really mean it or was he caught up in their weeklong flurry of eggnog and mistletoe, and hot monkey sex?

"What he's trying to say is he used to call me Ice Queen and I called him Mr. Perfect. I'd bet he didn't know my first name before Friday. Let's just say it's been a surprising week." Tell-tale heat crept into her cheeks.

Sam snorted. "Oh, I get it. I thought Holt was the biggest jerk on the planet when we met, I used to call him 'Mr. Too Hot Hollywood'. So we weren't exactly love at first sight either." She turned and pressed a loud kiss on her husband's cheek.

Love at first sight? Phoebe's breath caught in her now parched throat. Rafe reached for his race car token, leaving only cool air where his warm hand had been. She turned and looked at him, but he was studiously focused on the game board. Did everyone believe they were *in love?* Her stomach twisted, but she kept her casual smile pasted to her face.

Rafe gathered some pastel colored paper money and shoved it across the table. "Holt, I'd like to buy Park Place."

No acknowledgement nor reaction to the love comment.

She gulped a sip of wine. Maybe she was just overreacting, but she needed a moment to herself. Sure, they were spending Christmas together and they'd been attached at the hip since the Jingle Ball, but love? Marriage? Was this the conclusion his family had jumped to because she was the first woman he'd brought home for the holidays? Did *Rafe* believe she was in love with him?

She patted Rafe's leg and he glanced at her, his eyes guarded. "Can you let me up please?"

She stood and addressed everyone but him. "Where's the restroom?"

"It's the first door on the left when you walk out of the kitchen." Jake waved toward the hallway.

Phoebe bolted before her emotions betrayed her. Her compartmentalizing skills had deserted her. Rafael already had the upper hand because she was the one who had crushed on him in graduate school and he hadn't been aware of her existence. No matter what he said and no matter that he'd invited her here.

No way in hell would she allow herself to fall in love when she had no idea how deep Rafael's feelings went. And it was too soon to call it love. Right? More like being swept up in a holiday romance.

～

RAFE SHUFFLED and sorted his cash into neat piles after his purchase. Judging from Phoebe's practically sprinting out of the room, she also felt uncomfortable with the "L" word being tossed into the mix. He'd had the best week of his life with her, he liked her, he admired her, and he couldn't get enough of her in bed, but love?

"Okay, spill it." Jake leaned forward across the table.

Rafe glanced up and six pairs of eyes were glued expectantly on his face. He cleared his throat and reached for his wine. "Spill what?"

Amanda's brows rose. "Oh, come on, Rafe. You're totally different around her. You called her the most incredible woman you've ever met. You two have rainbows and hearts floating around your heads. She seems great. Is this it?"

"Yes, Rafael, are you finally going to get married?" Rafe's father, who apparently had the hearing of a bat, called from across the kitchen.

"Dad, I can't believe you said that to her. Stop." He held up his hands. "Look everyone, I like Phoebe a lot. Please don't make her uncomfortable, okay?" *Because I'm pretty damn uncomfortable now.* Why had he agreed to spend Christmas Eve with all of them again? Right now he could have been back on the rug in front of his fireplace with Phoebe's long silky legs wrapped around him. Just the two of them.

"Awww, he wants to make sure she feels comfortable. It's definitely love." Dylan sighed and clasped her hands together in front of her chest.

"Everyone. Stop. It's new. Can we leave it at that for tonight?" His pulse throbbed at his temples. It took a lot to embarrass him, but these people were relentless. It wasn't just his parents and brother anymore, there was an entire team chiming in with their opinions.

"Rafe." His brother's voice was quiet. "She seems amazing. Don't screw it up."

"He won't screw it up." Amanda smiled at him in her soothing way.

"Who won't screw what up?" Phoebe asked, suddenly standing beside the table.

"I won't screw up my lead in this game. I'm putting hotels on Park Place and Boardwalk and the bunch of you will be bankrupt before dinner." Rafe reached his hand out and tugged Phoebe down next to him. "Your turn."

They finished out the game and Rafe did indeed kick everyone's butts, including Samantha's, in record time, if he did say so himself. Thankfully nobody brought up love and he and Phoebe relaxed into fun flirtation again.

Sure, he wanted to slide his hands into her tumble of fiery waves. Sure, he savored every witty comment to fall from her tempting lips. Sure, he'd spent every free moment with her this week and it only made him want to continue seeing her. She was different than any woman he'd ever met. But they'd been seeing each other for less than one week––and they hadn't returned to the office since everything changed between them.

"Everyone to the table. And Rafe, if you want the seat of honor at the head of the table, please take it. You've earned us a one-year reprieve of Sam's singing." Chris laughed.

"Hey, I'm not that bad." Sam said and looked around. "Okay, maybe singing isn't one of my many talents, but you don't need to rub it in."

They settled around the table and dug into a feast of Cornish game hens and about a hundred side dishes, each one tastier than the next. Phoebe sat across from him, chatting with his mom seated next to her. She fit right in with the cheerful, loud group and the softness of her expression and frequency of her laugh made her appear even more gorgeous. How he'd ever seen her as a cold, rigid person seemed impossible now.

He couldn't wait to whisk her back to his house. She'd agreed to spend the night, so they'd spend Christmas morning together before heading to his parents' house for his chef father's signature holiday seafood feast. Their relationship was moving at warp speed, but right now, all signs were go, as long as his parents and the McNeills refrained from bringing up love again.

And no need to stress about returning to the office. Neither of them had allowed their personal lives to interfere with their professional lives before.

Phoebe glanced up, her eyes gleaming pewter behind her glasses and winked. He went rigid--thank god for the colorful fabric napkin disguising his instant arousal. Yeah, this portion of the night couldn't end soon enough.

CHAPTER 9

*P*hoebe placed the phone into its cradle, twirled around in her office chair, and threw her arms in the air in a victorious cheer. "Yes!"

Unable to suppress her glee, she popped up from her seat and danced around her office, adrenaline fueling her step-ball-change and cha-cha-chas. Yes, yes, yes--both clients she and Rafe had courted at the Jingle Ball had confirmed they were coming on board with Trident Wealth. Even more exhilarating than simply earning new business for the firm, both the Levines and the Samuels conditioned their acceptance on working exclusively with them as a team.

Now if on Friday afternoon before the Jingle Ball, someone had told her she'd be rejoicing at the prospect of partnering with Mr. Perfect, she'd have snorted her tea out her nose. No, she'd blazed her career path on her own and sharing the glory with Rafael wouldn't have been on the menu. Not that she wasn't a team player, but their rivalry precluded any desire to work together, even on a tiny project, much less sharing two prestigious clients.

How swiftly her perspective had altered over the last ten

days. After spending most of the prior week and the holidays with Mr. Rafael Cruz, somehow her solitary glory didn't seem quite so important. Of course, she planned on getting full credit for her efforts and that included full financial credit and the praise and respect of her boss. Now that she knew Rafe better––and wasn't that a euphemism––she had no issues sharing the success with him. A flash of all they'd shared together sent heat radiating down her spine and her lips curved up.

"Someone looks like the cat who swallowed the cream. Care to share?"

She glanced up and there he stood––all six foot something of sinewy grace silhouetted in her open doorway––a dangerous grin lighting up his handsome face. Her pulse kicked up another notch.

"Yes I do. We got both clients and they won't work with anyone but us––the 'dream team'." She laughed and pumped her fist in the air.

He crossed the space between them in two strides, caught her in his arms, and captured her mouth. She wrapped her arms around his neck and melted against him, savoring the strength of his lean frame. Heat shot straight to her center when his rigid arousal dug into her. He slid his hands up her back, one hand cupped the back of her head, and he deepened the kiss. Flames sparked along her skin and the rest of the world evaporated except for his clean masculine scent, the feel of him through the too many bothersome layers of clothing, and the taste of his breath mingling with hers.

"Ahem." Her assistant Cari cleared her throat. "Uh, Mr. MacDonald wanted to see you both in his office."

They leapt apart. Phoebe retreated a step and smoothed a strand of hair back in her chignon. "Of course, you can let him know we'll be right down."

Her assistant nodded, her eyes wide, and fled down the hall.

Awkward much? For a moment, Phoebe and Rafe stared at each other. Their newfound habit of kissing in inappropriate places needed to be curbed––pronto.

Rafe's dark brows drew together. "Isn't she the one who reported to MacDonald about the tea situation in the break room? Damn, do you think she'll gossip?"

Phoebe grimaced. "Probably. Especially since apparently everyone in the office knows we don't get along."

Rafe shook his head. "Didn't get along. I don't think that's the issue now. Do you want me to go speak with her before we go to Cliff's office?"

Phoebe ran her tongue around her teeth, weighing her options, and a spark of unease snaked down her spine. She couldn't be the only one feeling the unspoken tension over his family's reaction to them at Christmas. Rafe hadn't brought it up and she hadn't wanted to burst their bubble.

But would things change now they were back in the real world?

"And say what? I don't want her to feel uncomfortable or think she has to cover for us." Although they were equals at work, if anyone was criticized in this type of scenario, it was the woman. She'd spent her entire career ensuring nobody could question her integrity.

Rafe massaged the back of his neck. "True. I hadn't thought this through, but what you shared with me about maintaining your professional reputation stuck with me. I don't want us seeing each other to be a problem."

"Well, kissing in my office isn't exactly professional for either of us. But I think if anyone says anything, we just were excited about the new clients and hugged in a moment of impulse." Sounded like a bunch of b.s., but hey. "Although I'd rather not be the object of office gossip."

He rubbed his jaw. "I guess we need to discuss how to move forward, now that everything has changed."

Heat flushed Phoebe's cheeks. "Um, we haven't discussed much over the last few weeks." But the love and marriage comments on Christmas Eve needed to be addressed at some point.

His sober expression softened and he grinned. "Are you complaining?"

Her lips twitched. "Absolutely not, Mr. Cruz."

"I don't think there are rules against co-workers dating, but it's probably smarter if we keep it on the down low, at least for now. Okay?" One of his dark brows winged up.

Something tightened in Phoebe's chest. "You're right. So if asked directly if we're seeing each other, we say yes, but otherwise, keep it quiet?" Not that she wanted to run around yelling that they were going steady like in high school, but she wasn't one to sneak around either.

"Sounds good." The heat in his whiskey brown eyes deepened and a tingle shot through her remembering what usually happened when his eyes held that audacious gleam.

Phoebe's desk phone buzzed and she glanced down. "Crap, that's Cliff. We better head down there."

They strolled down the hallway to Cliff's office, electricity sparking between them. She scooted a little further away from him, gathering her composure. With so much unspoken and undecided between them, it was time to be all business.

Cliff's door was ajar. When they entered, their boss clapped his hands, a wide smile on his face. "Bravo, dream team. You two make me proud."

Rafe grinned. "We weren't sure if you'd spoken to them yet, but since you're using that term, I see you have."

Phoebe sank into the chair next to Rafe and bit the inside

of her lip to hide her smile. Did Rafe realize he'd referred to them in the plural? Would their boss?

"Sit down and let's discuss what this means for the firm and for you. I trust you both had a good holiday?" Cliff rested his chin on his steepled fingers and shifted his gaze between them, his brows raised. "Tell me everything."

Phoebe shifted in her seat, a trickle of perspiration popping up along the back of her neck. *Everything?* If he had any idea--the wine cave, Rafe's house, Christmas, her condo over the prior weekend...

"Best Christmas ever. And at the Jingle Ball? Phoebe was fantastic and had charmed them all before the main course was served. They didn't have a chance."

Cliff's eyebrows rose at Rafe's enthusiastic response. *Best Christmas ever? It definitely had been for her.* She glanced at Rafe, who was leaning forward, his corded muscular forearms resting on his thighs.

Phoebe smoothed her damp palms along her navy wool skirt. "Thank you, but Rafe is the charmer around here. To be frank, the evening went very smoothly. It wasn't difficult to establish rapport, their questions were straightforward, and I think they trust their friends. Our two joint conference calls last week ironed out their more specific questions."

Rafe nodded. "We worked well as a team."

Cliff studied them and Phoebe fought not to squirm under his scrutiny. Her pulse kicked up and she didn't dare look over at Rafe again.

"That's exactly what both of them told me--you two were charming and excellent partners. And I'm glad to hear it because my decision this year was going to be a tough one and now it's a moot point."

"A moot point?" Rafe and Phoebe spoke in unison.

Cliff nodded. "Exactly. I'd always assumed Rafe would take the reins when I retire, but then you appeared Phoebe, and my decision wasn't crystal clear any longer. Now that I know the two of you work well as a team, I can make you equal partners. Fifty-fifty. What do you think?"

"Equal partners?" Rafe said and turned to look at her, his eyes narrowed. "Does that work for you?"

She adjusted her glasses, stalled for time. "Does it work for you?"

An equal partnership could be the perfect solution. She'd receive what she'd bargained for when she'd moved to California to work for Trident Wealth. But what happened if or when they broke up? A stabbing pain dug into her belly.

He paused, his gaze locked with hers. "I think it's the perfect solution, if you agree to it."

She nodded. "I do." She broke the intensity of their shared gaze and looked at Cliff. "You aren't planning on retiring anytime soon, are you?"

Cliff laughed and shook his head. "Well, I've got to tell you I didn't want to come back from Aspen yesterday. I'm going to find a place and start splitting my time in the summer. But realistically, we're looking at six to twelve months, which will give us time to create a structure that works for everyone."

"Works for me." Once again Rafe and Phoebe spoke in unison.

Cliff's brows rose to his hairline. "You two are like different people. The Jingle Ball must have been quite a night. You saved me a major dilemma—this is the best news."

Phoebe cleared her throat to stifle the nervous laughter threatening to burst out. Cliff had no idea.

"You're right Cliff." Rafe stood. "It was quite a night and I know I see Phoebe in a whole new light."

Phoebe bit the inside of her cheek and rose from the chair. A whole new light indeed. "Thanks Cliff. Cari is setting up appointments for each new client and it would be great for you to pop in."

Cliff grinned. "Of course. And we're going to lunch down at George's to celebrate. I've got a patio table reserved at 1 p.m. Thanks for the excellent work."

They exited the room. "Will you come to my office for a moment? My assistant is still out of town, so we're safe." Rafe asked.

"That doesn't sound safe to me. Keep it professional Cruz, remember?" Her belly fluttered.

"Yeah, yeah, but I really want to see what you're wearing under that proper navy suit." He whispered and waggled his eyebrows.

"Wouldn't you love to know?" He'd left her apartment just after daybreak this morning, after they'd shared a long, steamy shower.

When they reached his corner suite, he closed the door behind them. "I hope to find out tonight. But we should talk before we go to lunch. Let's sit down."

"Talk." Her heartrate shot from stroll to gallop as she followed him to the small conference room table and chairs next to the floor-to-ceiling corner windows. "About the promotion or the last few weeks?"

"All of it." He moved his chair closer to hers so their knees almost grazed. She caught a hint of his crisp masculine scent.

She swallowed the nerves rising in her throat and worked to slow down her breathing. She gestured with one hand toward him. "You start."

His lips quirked. "Okay. I'm sorry about my dad and my sisters-in-law getting so personal on Christmas Eve. It was awkward."

She nodded. "Yes, it was, but it's not their fault. But now that we're back at work, we should probably set up some ground rules."

One black brow winged up and he chuckled. "You and your rules. Did you make a list?"

"Ha-ha. Very funny. It's just besides agreeing we'd keep it professional, we haven't discussed what we're doing and what happens if…" She gazed down at her clasped fingers.

Rafe caught her hands in his. "Phoebe, look at me."

She lifted her gaze to meet his and her breath lodged in her throat.

"I'm crazy about you. I've never felt this way before. I don't have all the answers. It's only been a few weeks, but I don't want it to end." Sincerity gleamed in his dark gaze.

Her heart performed a slow rolling dive through her chest. She turned her palms up and interlaced her fingers with his. "I feel exactly the same way, but what if--?"

Rafe leaned in closer. "We deal in 'what ifs' every day. That's what we do. We gamble. My gut tells me this gamble is worth any risk. And if somehow, something changes, we'll deal with it."

Phoebe bridged the last few inches separating them. "You're right. You're worth the risk."

She slid her hand into his thick hair and he captured her chin in one strong hand. Slowly, eyes wide open, they sealed the deal with a kiss.

ext December

RAFE PADDED SILENTLY across the plush carpet of the master bedroom's walk-in closet, two flutes of Cristal in his hands. Clad only in a silky black strapless bra, matching thong, and sky-high stilettos, Phoebe stood in front of the full-length mirror and fluffed her titian ringlets. He slid one arm around her narrow waist, nuzzled her neck, and inhaled her delicious vanilla scent.

She leaned against him. "Champagne before the ball, I like your style. I was about to get dressed and come downstairs, but this works too."

Her silky skin heated his bare torso and instantly, he was rock hard. "We've got a lot to celebrate tonight. It's our anniversary, so I couldn't wait."

She turned in his arms, raised one auburn brow, and accepted the glass. "The wine cave incident anniversary?

He tapped his champagne flute to hers. "Maybe we can

sneak in there again, make it an annual tradition?"

She toasted him and sipped the cool crisp drink. "Don't tempt me. What time is the car coming to pick us up? Do we have any time now?" She trailed her slender fingers down his chest, leaving a trail of goosebumps.

"The car will be here in twenty minutes. I need to ask you something before we go." He retreated a step, his heart kicking against his ribs, his mouth dry as the Sahara.

"I just need to throw on my dress and I'm ready. Is everything okay? You sound serious all of a sudden." Her silver eyes widened.

He took her champagne flute and set both glasses on the honeyed oak dresser. Phoebe tilted her head to one side and watched him. "Rafe?"

He dropped to one knee, clasped her ivory hands, and gazed up into her eyes. "Phoebe Hollingsworth, you changed my life last year in ways I could never have imagined. My dad told me that one day I'd meet *the* woman and I'd know immediately. All I know is that right away, you captured my interest with your intelligence and your strength. Then that red dress will forever be burned in my soul because you captured me with your beauty and your confidence. The wine cave sealed the fact that our chemistry was off the charts and deeper on every level.

"I don't want to only be your work partner, although we are the dream team. I love you with all my heart and want to spend the rest of our lives showing you how much. Will you marry me?"

Her scarlet lips were parted, her eyes were wide, and she tugged on his hands, pulling him back to standing. "I love you, Rafael Cruz. Even though we could have started this back at Harvard, I think everything worked out the way it was supposed to. Yes, absolutely yes!"

She threw her arms around his neck and he captured her

waist, spinning her across the wide expanse of his walk-in closet. "I planned to propose on Christmas Eve and I'm sorry to propose in the closet, but I couldn't wait."

"It doesn't matter where. I'm so happy, Rafe. But, umm, are you forgetting something?" Phoebe stopped and pressed her hands against his chest.

"I love you. I want to marry you. We're partners. I want you to move in now?" Rafe gazed down at her and laughed.

"Oh, you mean this?" In his haste to propose, he'd forgotten an important element. He reached into the pocket of his charcoal gray tuxedo pants and whipped out the robin's egg blue box.

Her small white teeth captured her full lower lip. "Well, I mean if we are making it official and all…"

"Oh, we are definitely making it official." He stepped back and flipped open the lid, revealing the cushion cut diamond set in a delicate antique platinum setting. "Will you officially marry me, Phoebe?"

She held out her hand and he slipped the ring on her finger.

"It fits perfectly. It is perfect, Rafe, and so are you. And I love you." She admired the engagement ring and then wrapped her arms around him.

Contentment and excitement battled for position in his heart. "I love you so much. Okay, we've got to go to the Jingle Ball."

She pressed one more kiss on his lips. "I didn't think we could top last year's event, but we already have before it started. If you'll zip me up, I'm ready to go."

She stepped into a tawny gold gown and turned her back so he could slide the zipper home. His fingers lingered on her soft skin and he pressed a kiss on her shoulder.

Hands linked, they sauntered downstairs to celebrate the rest of their lives.

WHAT'S NEXT

Two best friends. Only one bed during a blizzard...will one kiss change everything forever? Grant Michaels, the McNeill sisters' stepbrother is back in a friends to lovers, snowed-in steamy romance in *The Wonder of You*, Pacific Vista Ranch Book 5.

Click here to start reading **The Wonder of You** now. Or you can copy this link to your browser:

https://books2read.com/thewonderofyou

****

And if you have a moment, please leave a review for *Wrapped Up with You* on your favorite book site.

ALSO BY CLAIRE MARTI

Pacific Vista Ranch Series

Nobody Else But You

The Very Thought of You

For The Love of You

Wrapped Up with You

The Wonder of You

California Suits Series

Hotel King

Wine Country King

Monterey King

Holiday Queen

Palm Springs King

Romance in Laguna Beach Series

Second Chance in Laguna

At Last in Laguna

Sunset in Laguna

ACKNOWLEDGMENTS

When I wrote *The Very Thought of You*, Jake's older brother Rafael Cruz leapt onto the page and I knew he deserved his own book. The initial version of *Wrapped Up with You* was a short story in the USA Today Bestselling Jingle Balls anthology. I've expanded Rafe and Phoebe's story from 15k to 23k words because all their office rival, enemies to lovers fun deserved more time.

I'm grateful for all the assistance I received. Without all the input and support, I couldn't have done it! I want to thank my wonderful beta readers and critique partners: Kay Bennett, Joanna Kelly, Sara Martin, Lacy Pope, and Katie O'Sullivan—you each help me more than you could imagine. I appreciate your time and opinions.

To my wonderful editor, Lindsey Faber, thank you for helping me expand and polish this story. To my brother Robert Petretti––thanks for your love and support, both as my big brother and as proofreader extraordinaire.

Last but not least, to Todd for your patience and support. I love you. And, finally to my furry kids: Lola, Beau and Josie, thanks for providing me unconditional love.

ABOUT THE AUTHOR

Claire Marti is an award winning and *USA Today* Bestselling author of swoonworthy Contemporary Romance novels set in Southern California, including the Pacific Vista Ranch series and the Finding Forever in Laguna series. She lives in San Diego with her husband, silly dog, and three clever cats.

Claire started writing stories as soon as she was old enough to pick up pencil and paper. After graduating from the University of Virginia with a BA in English Literature, Claire was sidetracked by other careers, including practicing law, selling software for legal publishers, and managing a non-profit animal rescue for a Hollywood actress.

Finally, Claire followed her heart and now focuses on two of her true passions: writing romance and teaching yoga.

facebook.com/ClaireMartiAuthor

instagram.com/clairemartiwrites

amazon.com/Claire-Marti/e/B01N9VOWLL

bookbub.com/profile/claire-marti

goodreads.com/clairemarti

tiktok.com/@clairemartiwrites

www.ingramcontent.com/pod-product-compliance
Lightning Source LLC
Chambersburg PA
CBHW021205110726
47900CB00002B/738